THE Sisters 8

BOOK 7

REBECCA'S RASHNESS

By Lauren Baratz-Logsted
With Greg Logsted & Jackie Logsted
Illustrated by Lisa K. Weber

sandpiper

HOUGHTON MIFFLIN HARCOURT

BOSTON • NEW YORK • 2011

Text copyright © 2011 by Lauren Baratz-Logsted,
Greg Logsted, and Jackie Logsted

Illustrations copyright © 2011 by Lisa K. Weber

For information about permission to reproduce selections from this book,
write to Permissions, Houghton Mifflin Harcourt Publishing Company,
215 Park Avenue South, New York, New York 10003.

www.hmhbooks.com

The text of this book is set in Youbee.
Book design by Carol Chu.

Library of Congress Cataloging-in-Publication Data
Baratz-Logsted, Lauren.
Rebecca's rashness/by Lauren Baratz-Logsted with Greg Logsted and Jackie Logsted.
p. cm.—(The sisters eight ; bk. 7)
Summary: When Rebecca demonstrates superhuman strength she brings unwanted
publicity to the Huit octuplets, but much greater danger is in store when she
acquires the power to shoot fire from her fingertips.
[1. Abandoned children—Fiction. 2. Sisters—Fiction. 3. Humorous stories.]
I. Logsted, Greg. II. Logsted, Jackie. III. Title.
PZ7.B22966Reb 2011
[Fic]—dc22
2010039256

ISBN 978-0-547-55433-4 paper over board
ISBN 978-0-547-55434-1 paperback

Manufactured in the United States of America
DOC 10 9 8 7 6 5
4500354473

For Betsy Groban:
Thank you for publishing our series.

Annie   Durinda   Georgia   Jackie

Marcia   Petal   Rebecca   Zinnia

PROLOGUE

Hello again.

I'd have put an exclamation point after that but I'm not feeling very exclamatory at the moment. Then again, neither are most of the Eights.

Dread. Now there's a word for the old vocabulary list. *Dread,* a noun meaning "a great fear, especially in the face of impending evil." *Dread*—we'll get back to this shortly.

I suppose you're wondering what will happen to the Eights next. "And then what happened?"—this is the question that has driven storytellers for centuries, for millennia even. It's the question that drives readers to turn to the next page.

But before we begin turning pages, we must once again do a brief recap for those of you who have been away from the story for a few months, although the story itself is ongoing even in your absence.

Very well.

The Huit octuplets need to figure out what happened to their parents, those parents who so inconveniently disappeared around ten o'clock at night on December 31, 2007. But before they can do that, each sister must discover her own individual power and gift. Thus far, six of the eight sisters have done their parts.

Annie: power — can think like an adult when
  necessary; gift — purple ring
Durinda: power — can freeze people, except Zinnia;
  gift — green earrings
Georgia: power — can become invisible; gift — gold
  compact
Jackie: power — faster than a speeding train;
  gift — red cape
Marcia: power — X-ray vision; gift — purple cloak
Petal: power — can read people's minds; gift — silver
  charm bracelet

Two of the Eights, Rebecca and Zinnia, have yet to do their parts. And that is the problem currently facing the Eights. You see, like you, they would like to get on with the story. They would love, perhaps even more than you, to discover the answer to the burning question "And then what happened?" They'd particularly like to know that because at the end of *Book 6: Petal's Problems,* some new and interesting information came to light.

But what happens next may be a big problem:

Rebecca is next.

Oh, if only Zinnia were next, seven of them say to themselves, particularly Zinnia. I can't say I disagree. If Zinnia were next, everything would be sweetness and light; adorable Zinnia cares hardly at all about getting her power and mostly focuses on her gift. Oh, if only the Eights could leapfrog right over July and into August.

Unfortunately, time doesn't work that way. There is a natural order of things even when dealing with an unnatural creature such as Rebecca.

Durinda might have been concerned about the nature of her power, but Petal is the only Eight to ever flat-out not want hers.

Well, seven out of eight Eights polled don't want Rebecca to have her power.

And now we come full circle to . . .

Dread.

Let the fireworks, as they say, begin.

ONE

We would have liked to be solving the mysteries of the universe, or at least the mysteries of our universe. In particular, we would have liked to be focusing on the recently acquired knowledge that, in addition to having a crazy younger sister, our missing mother had an identical twin named Queen. In super-particular, we would have liked to be focusing on the fact that Queen and her husband, Joe Ocho, had some offspring, number unspecified, that we had strong reason to believe were those ominous beings known as the Other Eights.

But we couldn't do any of that, could we?

We couldn't do any of that because (1) we were asleep, it being that time period ridiculously referred to as "the middle of the night" — ridiculous because dead in the middle of the period most people are asleep, night formally becomes morning; (2) we had something more immediate that was weighing on at least seven of our minds, even if those minds were currently slumbering;

and (3) just as the clock turned over to 12:01 a.m. on July 1, seven of us were rudely awakened by the sound of "Hup one! Hup two!" shouted from below.

We tried to ignore it. We really did. Some of us needed our beauty rest, some of us needed that night-time respite from the active duty of daily life to regroup for the next day, and one of us was still recovering from having a monthlong nervous breakdown over getting her power. But try as we might to ignore the shouts of "Hup one!" and "Hup two!"—not to mention all sorts of annoying pounding noises—after fifteen minutes we realized we'd never get back to sleep under these conditions, so we went to investigate.

We found Rebecca hanging by her arms from the chandelier.

Rebecca had on workout sweats, even though it was the dead of summer and the dead of night, and a sweatband around her head. As we watched, she used her arms to pull her body upward.

"What are you doing?" Annie demanded.

"And here you think you're so smart," Rebecca said, chinning herself again over the edge of the chandelier. "What does it look like I'm doing? I'm doing pull-ups."

"But it's the middle of the night," Georgia objected.

"Technically," Marcia corrected, "even though it won't be light for another five or six hours, it's morning."

Six of us stared at Marcia. We respected that she was the most observant among us, but she could be so annoyingly precise at times and we were cranky from being woken up.

"Sorry." Marcia blushed. "Sometimes I just can't help myself."

"Middle of the night, beginning of the morning—

who cares?" Rebecca said. Then she dropped to the ground and began doing pushups. "Hup one! Hup two!" We were shocked to see that Rebecca could push herself up so hard that she was able to clap her hands together neatly before beginning the next pushup.

Jackie was the fastest of us, in terms of sheer physical speed, but we were quite certain even she couldn't do this pushup thing the way Rebecca was now doing it.

"I could see that you were doing pull-ups on the chandelier when we first came in," Jackie said in a reasonable tone of voice, "and I can see that now you are doing hand-clap pushups. Oops! You just switched to jackknife sit-ups — that was fast! But what I don't think any of us understands is . . . why?"

"Hup one! Hup two!" Rebecca rose from the floor and began sprinting around the room, talking as she sprinted. We must say, our heads got a little dizzy trying to keep track of her progress. In particular, Petal grew very dizzy, as did our eight cats — Anthrax, Dandruff, Greatorex, Jaguar, Minx, Precious, Rambunctious, and Zither — who'd just entered the room, no doubt awakened by all the clatter and clamor Rebecca was creating. Well, Rambunctious didn't remain dizzy for long because soon Rambunctious was sprinting along with her mistress.

"What I'm doing," Rebecca said, "which should be

obvious, is getting myself in shape. You know — preparing my body to receive my power."

"You're doing . . . *what?*" Annie demanded.

"Getting in shape, preparing my body," Rebecca said. "Did you not hear me the first time?"

"We heard you," Georgia said. "But you're not making any sense. This is the middle of the night." Immediately after speaking the words, she raised her hand in Marcia's direction in a stopping gesture. Georgia was right to do that, for Marcia's mouth was already open to speak. "This is the very dark beginning of the morning and none of us sees any reason why you should be doing this right now."

"None of you sees." Rebecca sneered as she sprinted. "Of course none of you sees. But that's because none of you was ready to receive her power. Annie didn't even know she had hers until Georgia pointed it out. Durinda had to be shown a pro-and-con list for hers. Georgia didn't figure out for the longest time what use hers was. Marcia's gave her headaches. And Petal." Rebecca added a snort to go with the sneer and the sprint. "We all know how *that* turned out."

"You didn't mention Jackie," Zinnia pointed out.

"No, I didn't," Rebecca said. And then Rebecca gave Jackie a look of grudging admiration. "That's because you're different somehow. Your power of speed just came on you and you slid right into it as though you were born to it." Rebecca paused, then shrugged off whatever admiration she might have been feeling for another being. "Still, fitting a power like a glove is nothing like what it'll be for me. Because I will be totally prepared, ready to embrace whatever may come."

"Oh, bother." Georgia rolled her eyes.

We couldn't blame her. What Rebecca was saying was very eye-roll-worthy. Why did she have to be so melodramatic about this? In her own way, she was even worse than Petal about this stuff!

Rebecca finally stopped running.

"I think I need a high-protein snack," Rebecca said. "Durinda, make one for me, won't you? There's my good girl."

"I'm not your good girl," Durinda said, clearly highly offended, which proves it never pays to talk down to the household cook. "It's the middle of the night." Durinda shot a look at open-mouthed Marcia. "It's the beginning of the morning. My kitchen is closed."

"Fine." Rebecca shrugged. "I can make something myself."

Rebecca marched into the kitchen, Rambunctious by her side, and we followed behind. We may have been exhausted and exasperated, but we were curious as to what Rebecca would consider a high-protein snack.

Once in the kitchen, Rebecca opened the refrigerator.

"You're not Durinda," Carl the talking refrigerator immediately objected, although he did sound groggy.

"No, I'm not, Carl," Rebecca said, removing a carton of eggs. "I'm prettier and smarter."

"I don't know if I'd say all that," Carl said. "I only have eyes for robot Betty. But you are ruder. Durinda would never wake me in the middle of the night like this." Immediately, Carl added, "Sorry, Marcia, I mean the beginning of the morning."

Marcia closed her mouth as Rebecca closed the refrigerator door and Carl fell silent.

We fell silent too as we watched Rebecca take a glass from the cabinet, remove an egg from the carton, crack the egg on the side of the glass, drop the raw egg into the glass, toss the shell on the counter, remove another egg from the carton —

·7·

"What are you planning on doing with that?" Annie demanded.

"That is *not,*" Durinda pointed out, "how you make scrambled eggs. When I scramble eggs I use a bowl, not a glass, to mix the eggs before pouring them into the prepared skillet. You haven't even prepared the skillet!"

We could tell Durinda was really mad at Rebecca, probably because of that crack about being prettier and smarter. Also because Rebecca had presumed to tell Durinda to make her a snack and now she was making a mess of Durinda's kitchen.

"That's because I'm not going to use a skillet," Rebecca said, dropping the contents of yet another cracked egg into the glass. How many eggs did this make? Five? Six? More? We were tempted to ask Marcia, who had superior math skills, but we were too busy wondering what Rebecca was going to do with that tall glass of raw egg.

We didn't have to wait long as Rebecca raised the glass toward her lips and—

"You can't drink that!" Petal said, leaping forward in her granny nightie—Petal would wear a granny nightie, even in summer—and grabbing on to Rebecca's arm. "That's *death!*"

"It's not certain death." Rebecca shrugged. "Only the threat of it." She tried to raise the glass to her lips again but Petal hung on tight.

"Petal's right, you know," Zinnia said.

Petal's right — those were words heard in our world as rarely as the words *Rebecca's right*. Still . . .

"It is very dangerous to eat raw eggs," Zinnia went on. "Weren't you paying attention in health class the last few years?"

"So?" was all Rebecca had to say to that.

"I didn't save your life in France," Petal said, still hanging on to Rebecca's raised arm, Petal's feet not even touching the ground now, "only to have you throw it away by raw-egging yourself to death."

"I don't care about any of that," Rebecca said. "I only care about getting my power and being ready for it when it comes."

Then, with Petal still hanging on, Rebecca managed to raise the glass the rest of the way to her lips.

It should have told us something, the way Rebecca was still able to raise her arm with Petal hanging on to it with her full weight, but it didn't in the moment. In the moment, we were too mesmerized by the sight of Rebecca glugging back that entire glass of raw egg without stopping once.

When she was done, she put the glass on the counter. After Petal finally slid off her arm, Rebecca used the back of her hand to wipe the egg mustache from her mouth.

"See?" Rebecca smiled at Petal. "I'm not dead yet."

"Perhaps not, but you could be by morning," Petal said, at once out-darking Rebecca.

"Petal simply means by the time it turns light out," Zinnia informed Marcia, who had to shut her mouth once again.

"I don't think I'll be dead by the time it turns light," Rebecca said. "In fact, between all the exercise and the raw eggs, I'm feeling stronger already."

Then Rebecca cracked her knuckles—what an awful sound!—and tilted her head back and stretched her arms wide to address the heavens, or at least our kitchen ceiling.

"Universe," Rebecca called triumphantly, "I'm ready for my power! You can send it to me anytime now!"

"Oh, bother," Georgia said.

"The rest of us are going back to bed," Annie announced. "Are you coming with us, Rebecca?"

"I don't think so," Rebecca said. "I haven't done my deep knee bends yet."

"Suit yourself," Annie said. "But if you're going to be saying 'Hup one!' and 'Hup two!' I think we'd all appreciate it if you'd whisper your *hup*s. Just because you're intent on being crazy, you don't have to drag us down too."

"Fair enough," Rebecca admitted.

As seven of us trooped back upstairs, we could hear a whispered "Hup one! Hup two!" coming from below.

"Rebecca will be fine, right?" Petal said worriedly.

"Probably," Zinnia said.

"Raw eggs might easily kill another girl," Marcia said, "so I hope other kids at home never try that stunt."

"But Rebecca's Rebecca," Georgia said. "A raw egg would be too scared to kill Rebecca. The egg would worry that somehow she could kill it back."

"Rebecca better clean up my kitchen when she's done," Durinda said, "or I'll kill her worse than any egg could."

"Durinda!" Annie admonished. "We never talk about killing one another, not even if we're talking about Rebecca."

"I suppose I'm glad that Rebecca will not be another egg victim," Petal said. "But that wasn't what I meant. When I asked if Rebecca will be fine, I meant when she finally gets her power. She will be, right?"

That's when Jackie put her arm kindly around Petal's shoulders and Annie said, "You're kidding, aren't you? Once Rebecca gets her power, I doubt any of us will ever be fine again."

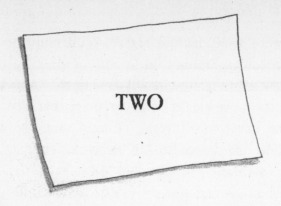

TWO

In the morning, when it was really morning, meaning actually light outside, seven of us woke up exhausted. What with the interrupted sleep we'd had the night before, it was all we could do to drag our sorry selves downstairs for breakfast.

Rebecca, on the other hand, looked completely fresh when we found her once again hanging from the chandelier. She looked as though she'd slept for a week, even though we were fairly certain she'd never even gone back to bed.

She also looked really impatient.

"I can't believe it's eight hours into July already and still my power hasn't arrived yet," Rebecca said. "What can be taking it so long?"

"Cool your jets," Petal told her.

We suspected Petal had been waiting her whole life to say something so rude to Rebecca.

"It'll get here in its own good time," Annie said.

"Yeah," Georgia said. "Like my gift coming too early and then me sending it back and then having to wait until the end of the month for it to make its way to me again. There's no point in trying to tamper with these things."

"Yeah," Durinda said, "so cool your jets."

We suspected that Durinda had also waited a long time to say something like that to Rebecca.

Durinda stretched, yawned. "Time for me to start breakfast. Jackie?"

Jackie yawned, stretched, and went with Durinda into the kitchen to help. The rest of us followed. We were very hungry, so hungry we might not even wait for Durinda and Jackie to put breakfast on the table but would eat it standing up as soon as it was ready.

"I think we'll have eggs today," Durinda said, "except we'll cook ours."

"Sorry to disappoint you," Carl the talking refrigerator said when Durinda opened the door, "particularly since you are always kind to me, Durinda, not like some rude people whose names I will not name, but there are no eggs left."

"I don't mean to contradict you, Carl," Durinda said, "but how is that possible? There was at least a whole carton here last night."

"That rude person whose name I will not name drank them all," Carl said.

"Rebecca!" We all turned on her.

"Rebecca," Annie said sternly, "I cannot believe you drank a dozen raw eggs."

"You will surely die now," Petal warned Rebecca. "I suppose I shall be very sad, but at least I will not be tempted to eat raw eggs, what with there no longer being any eggs in the house."

"You would never be tempted to eat raw eggs anyway," Marcia pointed out.

"You're much too cautious," Georgia said. "Why, you could never enjoy being caught in an avalanche the way I did."

"True and true," Petal admitted freely. "I'm the biggest scaredy-cat ever and proud of it."

"The cats have informed me," Zinnia said, "that they wish the term *scaredy-cat* to be retired forever. They say it casts aspersions on their character and that anyway, Precious is the only cat it's true of."

We ignored our loony littlest sister, all except for Jackie.

"Did the cats really use the word *aspersions*?" Jackie wanted to know.

Zinnia nodded.

"That's a very good word," Jackie said in a complimentary fashion. "I hope they're impressed with themselves."

"Jackie," Rebecca said, "why must you always insist on humoring—"

"That's enough out of you," Durinda told Rebecca. "Because of you, I can't make eggs as I had planned. Now, what can I make instead . . ."

"I'm sorry to inform you," Carl the talking refrigerator said, "but we are currently out of all breakfast items. After that rude person whose name I refuse to name finished with the eggs, she drank all the milk and the calcium-enriched orange juice, and then she broiled a steak."

It was then Durinda noticed the dirty broiler sitting in the sink.

"Couldn't you have cleaned up after yourself?" she asked Rebecca.

"I was too busy getting in shape," Rebecca said. "You know, I need to be prepared for my—"

"Power," Annie finished wearily. "Yes, we all do know."

"We could just have cereal then," Durinda said cheerily, trying to put a bright face on things.

"'Fraid not," Carl said. "Family history teaches that you don't like dry cereal, you all complain if you have to eat it, plus—"

"I know, I know." Durinda sighed. "Rebecca ate all the Razzle Crunchies, right?"

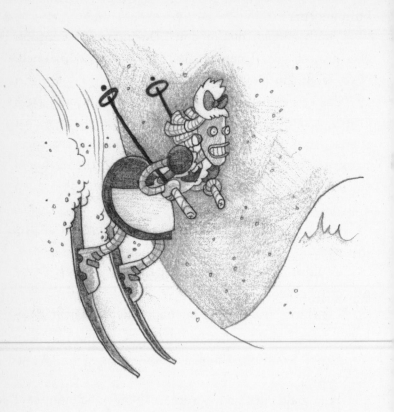

"Um, no," Carl said. "Robot Betty was watching a late-night movie. She didn't like the way the romance was going so she threw cereal at the TV in protest, then she crunched it with her metal feet. I told her she should vacuum up her mess—what would your mother say if she suddenly returned?—but instead robot Betty just went to Winter and took a few runs down the ski slope there."

Leave it to robot Betty. Our inventor-scientist mother had created her to make our lives easier, but instead she did things like throw all the Razzle Crunchies at the TV, leaving the cleanup for us, and then go skiing in Winter, one of the four seasonal rooms our mother had created so we could go to whatever season we wanted to be in at any given time.

"You know how Betty is," Carl added.

We did. Still, we loved her.

"Is there anything to eat for breakfast, Carl," Durinda asked, "that Rebecca hasn't eaten or Betty thrown?"

"Sorry," Carl said. "You really do need to do a Big Shop."

A *Big Shop* was what Mommy always called it when she needed to stock up on food and supplies for our somewhat large family. Thinking of the way Mommy always said that made us sad, missing her. Would we ever see her again? Or Daddy? But then . . .

"Annie," Zinnia piped up, "could we go on the Big Shop with you? You almost always do these things yourself, but this time it sounds like we need a Really Big Shop. It could be like an outing, and I should very much like to go on an outing because *that* would practically feel like getting a present."

Talking to animals and worrying about presents — it

was easy to see what Zinnia would focus on when it was finally her turn to have her own month. Zinnia was such a two-note girl. But then it occurred to us: sometimes we were all one- or two-note girls.

"It would be nice to get out of the kitchen," Durinda said.

"It's not fair to deny us the chance to go on a Really Big Shop," Georgia complained.

"I'm fine with it either way," Jackie said.

"While we're there," Marcia said, and then she cast a hasty glance at Annie and added, "*if* we do all go, it'd be fun and educational to calculate the number of square inches each item takes up on the shelf."

"I would like to go on an outing too," Petal said, "but what if I am walking by a pyramid display of cans of creamed corn and there is a slight earthquake, toppling the pyramid on top of me and crushing me to death? I can't think of a worse way to go, death by creamed corn, at least not at the moment."

"Can I push the cart?" Zinnia asked, raising her hand and waving it in Annie's face. For a minute there, Zinnia reminded us of our classmate Mandy Stenko. We almost missed Mandy, whom we hadn't seen since school got out in June, and we absolutely missed Will Simms, whom we hadn't seen in just as long a period of time. As for Principal McG and her husband, who'd come to teach us — the Mr. McG — the jury was still out on whether we missed them or not.

"Pleasepleaseplease!" Zinnia waved her hand in Annie's face some more.

Annie ignored her. We'd all learned there were times when the most sensible thing to do was ignore Zinnia. This was also true of Georgia, Petal, and Rebecca, who were often ignorable. We couldn't ignore Durinda because we needed her to cook for us. And it was almost impossible to ignore Marcia because she was so precise about everything, it somehow made us pay attention even if we didn't want to. Jackie never said or did anything that needed ignoring. As for Annie, we knew that if we tried to ignore her, we'd pay for it in the end.

"What about you?" Annie turned to Rebecca. "Don't you want to go on this thing the others are all so excited about, this thing they're calling a Really Big Shop?"

"No," Rebecca said. "I'd rather stay here and prepare for my—"

"Too bad," Annie cut her off, "because we're all going."

"Why can't I stay here alone?" Rebecca said, hands on hips.

Seven of us rolled our eyes. Surely Rebecca must be joking.

"It's one thing for eight of us to live alone without adult supervision," Annie said, "because we take care of one another. Somehow our strengths and weaknesses balance out. But to have any one of us stay here alone? And particularly *you?*" Annie shook her head. "That really would be chaos."

"Fine," Rebecca grumbled, "but can we make this Really Big Shop really quick? I need to get back here to prepare for my—"

"Power," Annie finished. "Yes, yes, we all know. We'll try to make it as quick as we can. Let me just go slip into my Daddy disguise, the one I use when I drive the Hummer, and then we'll be off."

"I suppose the rest of us should get changed too," Durinda said.

"We are all still in our jammies," Marcia observed.

We headed toward the stairs.

"Can I wear my jammies to the store?" Petal said, fingering the silver charm bracelet that she never took off, not even when she went to sleep. "I do feel safer with bunny slippers on my feet. They might protect me against a creamed-corn catastrophe."

It was hard for any of us, even Zinnia, who loved anything to do with animals, to imagine how bunny slippers could protect a person, much less keep someone from being crushed to death.

"Sorry, Petal," Annie said, "not this time. People already think our family is crazy enough without adding bunny-slippers-while-grocery-shopping into the mix." Annie paused for a moment, sniffed the air. "Rebecca," she said, "please change out of those sweaty clothes before we leave the house. You smell like a gym."

"Fine, fine," Rebecca grumbled some more. Then she consulted her workout watch. "I just can't believe we're eight hours and forty-three minutes into July and I still haven't—"

"July!" Petal shrieked, and for once her shriek was one of joy. "It's July, it's July, *it's July!*"

"Yes," Annie said, "I believe that fact has been established, more than once."

"My month, June, is officially over!" Petal crowed. "I can no longer read other people's thoughts! If Georgia is thinking, 'Petal's a little idiot,' I have no direct knowledge of that fact. Yippee!"

We all looked at Petal. Had there ever been an Eight who wanted her power less? Of course there hadn't.

"Plus," Petal went on breathlessly, "Rebecca hasn't received her power yet. So right now we're living in a world where no one has any powers." She shot a quick look at Annie and added, "Well, except for Annie with her power to think like an adult when necessary, but there's nothing scary about that. A world where no one has power—yippee!"

With that, Petal began spinning in happy circles on

the stair where she stood, which was a very dangerous thing to do since she almost fell off the stair.

"Oh, bother," Georgia said, propping Petal up to prevent her fall. "The little idiot's spun herself into a regular tizzy."

"I heard that!" Petal said. "Wait a second. Did you say that out loud, or am I still somehow reading your mind, or did I perhaps even just imagine it?"

"Anyway," Rebecca said, ignoring Petal, "I'm sure my getting my power is just a matter of time. And I'm sure once I do get it, it will be what Zinnia likes to refer to as a doozy."

Then she cracked her knuckles again.

That was when six of us began wishing she'd just hurry up and get her power, no matter how bad her getting it might turn out to be for the rest of us, because that sound was giving us the willies.

Tizzies, doozies, willies.

We really were quite a bunch.

We only hoped that with all these tizzies, doozies, and willies everything wouldn't suddenly go kablooey.

THREE

Annie pulled the car into the lot outside of the Super-Duper Food Extravaganza Shop That Sells Everything Else Too Including Gilded Birdcages.

Every time we looked at that sign we thought that if a person lettered signs for a living, after painting just that one sign, he or she could retire as a millionaire and go live in the Bahamas.

The lot was so full, Annie had to drive around for a bit before finding a parking spot. What was going on here? Had everyone in the whole world decided to go shopping on the same day we had?

"Did you notice the Hummer was making a pinging noise as we drove over here?" Marcia observed.

"I don't think cars are supposed to go *ping!* like that," Petal said. "What if some evil person has programmed our car to make a special noise that will slowly drive us all insane?"

"I don't think it's anything to worry about," Annie

said, readjusting her Daddy mustache, which had tilted at an odd angle. "Let's shop, shall we?"

Once we were inside the store, whose name we would repeat here if only it weren't so long, Annie directed Zinnia to get a cart.

"And please get the giganto one," Annie said. "It's the only one big enough to hold everything our family needs."

Zinnia did as asked and fetched the giganto cart, which was the only one of its size.

"Okay," Annie said, "let's split up so this is organized and doesn't take us all day. Georgia and Rebecca, you handle the fresh produce, bread, and baked goods. Durinda and Jackie, you take care of boxed and canned goods plus frozen foods. Petal and Zinnia, you get the meats and pet supplies. Marcia and I will get beverages and cleaning products and such."

"Okay," Zinnia said, "but don't be surprised if we come back with all fish. I'm thinking we should become pescatarians, people who eat fish but no meat. It's the cats' suggestion. They say they're uncomfortable with us eating animals that can walk on four legs."

"Can we get a birdcage?" Petal asked.

"No," Annie said.

"But this splitting-up system doesn't make sense," Georgia objected. "If Zinnia's the one with the cart, what are the rest of us supposed to do?"

"When your arms are full," Annie said, "you go find Zinnia and dump your items in the cart, then you go back for more."

"You didn't assign anyone the task of getting pink frosting," Rebecca pointed out.

"By all means," Annie said, "add it to your and Georgia's list. I'm sure we'd all hate for you to starve. Okay, gang." Annie clapped her hands. "Let's go divide and conquer."

It felt odd splitting up, since we were almost always all eight together everywhere, unless one of us got temporarily taken by an evil person or some such. Still, who knew what great things we might accomplish if we did this divide-and-conquer thing Annie was suggesting?

* * * * * * * *

"Do you think Annie will notice if we slip a birdcage into the cart?" Petal asked as Zinnia struggled with a twenty-five-pound bag of kibble, finally stowing it in the bottom of the cart.

"Yes," Zinnia said, a little out of breath from her efforts. "What do you want a birdcage for anyway? The only birds we ever have around the place are the carrier pigeons that come bearing notes, and I doubt any of them would enjoy living in a cage."

"I don't know," Petal said. "Haven't you ever wanted anything just for the sake of wanting it?"

Now this was something Zinnia could understand.

"All the time," Zinnia confessed freely. "Okay, what's next?"

"Meats," Petal said, "or I suppose fish since you said we shouldn't eat meat anymore."

"Do you think the cats would also object to us eating fish?" Zinnia wondered aloud. "After all, fish are animals too."

"I don't see why," Petal said. "Cats would eat fish all the time if they could get it, so I don't see why they would object to us doing it. Of course, cats will eat spiders too if they can get them but I don't think I want to try spider pizza anytime soon."

"Good point," Zinnia said.

* * * * * * * *

"There are so many different kinds of orange juice," Marcia observed. "Calcium-enriched, pulp, some pulp, no pulp — how is a person to decide?"

"You're right," Annie said. "It is a bit much. Georgia and Rebecca are getting the fresh produce. I'm sure they'll get oranges because Georgia always likes to practice juggling with them. She says it's good practice for the day we're all forced to join the circus. Perhaps

Durinda can just squeeze fresh for us this week? How much extra work can that be?"

* * * * * * * *

"Georgia," Rebecca said, "would you stop juggling those oranges and get a move on? We need to get home so I can continue with preparing for my—"

"Yes, yes." Georgia cut her off. "What's next on the list?"

"Bread and baked goods," Rebecca replied.

A few minutes later, as Rebecca and Georgia debated the merits of plain bagels versus flavored ones, a smell drifted by that was very familiar and much hated:

Fruitcake.

Rebecca's and Georgia's heads snapped up in time to see our evil toadstool of a neighbor, the Wicket, placing a fruitcake in a cart that was already filled to over-brimming with fruitcakes.

The Wicket's head snapped up in time to catch them looking.

"Petal, Zinnia," she said in greeting.

What a double mistake to make! The Wicket never could get us straight.

Naturally, Rebecca and Georgia glared at her over this.

"Stop looking at me like that!" the Wicket said, wheel-

ing her cart around and hurrying away. "Your whole family freaks me out!"

* * * * * * * *

Durinda's arms were filled with boxes of Razzle Crunchies and Jackie's were filled with cans of tuna and crushed pineapple as they rounded a corner and ran smack into the McG and the Mr. McG.

"Hello, Eights," the McG said. "Or should I say two-eighths?"

"I hope you're all spending your summer studying math, lying in hammocks, and staring up at clouds," the Mr. McG said.

"We have to go now," Durinda said.

"Bye!" Jackie said.

It was always so odd, seeing educators outside of school.

"Did you notice the Mr. McG was holding the McG's hand?" Durinda giggled. "It was so sweet. Of course, I'm mostly never sure if they even like each other."

"Does it seem to you like everyone in the world is here today?" Jackie wondered.

"If Petal were here right now," Durinda said, "she'd probably say, 'Oh no! If everyone in the world is here today, then all the evil people must be here too!'"

Yes. Yes, she would.

* * * * * * * *

We all finally met up at the line of registers.

"What do you think of making fresh-squeezed orange juice this week?" Annie asked Durinda.

"Are you sure we can't find room in our house for one small birdcage?" Petal asked.

"I've finally calculated how many square inches various items in this store take up," Marcia said, "just in case anyone wants to know."

"Can someone help me get this bag of kibble on the conveyor belt?" Zinnia asked, struggling under the weight of it.

"We saw the McG and the Mr. McG holding hands," Jackie said.

"It was shockingly sweet," Durinda said.

"We saw the Wicket hogging up all the fruitcake," Georgia said.

"But I'm pretty sure our mere presence scared her off," Rebecca said, dropping an armload of cans of pink frosting into Zinnia's giganto cart. Then she added, "Why is this line taking so long? Don't people realize I need to get home in order to—"

That's the moment we noticed the back of the head of the person standing in front of us, a hairless head, like one of the eggs from the carton last night before Rebecca cracked it open and drank it raw.

Principal Freud.

Or should we say *Frank* Freud, since he was no longer our principal.

"I thought you said he was going to Australia," Annie said in an urgent hushed whisper to Jackie.

"He was," Jackie said. "He did."

But evil always returned. We should have known that by now. It happened with Crazy Serena, it happened with the Wicket, and now it was happening with Frank Freud.

Just when you think it's safe to go shopping again . . .

Frank Freud must have sensed sixteen eyes staring at the back of his head, because he turned then.

We were sure he was shocked to see us there. And we were sure that he was really shocked to see Annie wearing a man's suit, a fedora, and a false mustache.

But we knew he wouldn't rat her out. Like all evil people we'd encountered, he'd learned to be somewhat fearful of us.

Still, running out of food, running into the Wicket, running into Frank Freud . . .

What else could possibly go wrong in our world today?

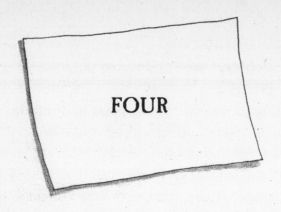

FOUR

"You know what's odd?" Annie said after we were all safely buckled in and she'd put the key in the ignition and started the car.

"Let's see," Marcia said, "odd . . . well, there's one, of course, and then there's three, five, you wouldn't want to forget seven, and then nine, eleven—"

"You," Rebecca added with a sneer toward Marcia, cutting off the numerical onslaught.

"Yes," Annie conceded, "half the numbers in the world and Marcia are odd, as are we all, but what I was referring to was the smoke pouring out the back of the Hummer."

"Smoke!" Petal screamed, unbuckling herself and throwing her little body from the car. "We're on fire!"

Petal's reaction may have been viewed as extreme by some people—okay, by all of us—but the smoke pouring out of the back of the Hummer was alarming, meaning that even the bravest among us eventually flung her body from the Hummer.

"I wonder if it has anything to do with that pinging noise I heard earlier?" Marcia said, scratching her head.

"We're all going to die!" Petal screamed, hurling her little body to the ground and covering her head with her hands, causing passersby to stare at us.

"This is bad," Jackie said. And for Jackie to say that, we all realized, it *must* be bad. "For the Hummer to be belching dark smoke when Mommy retooled the Hummer so that it would be an environmentally friendly vehicle . . . Well, let's just say it doesn't look environmentally friendly at the moment."

"I'll call for help," Annie said, opening the door of the Hummer and reaching inside for the car phone.

"Don't!" Petal screamed. "You could die!"

"It's just her arm, you little idiot," Georgia pointed out. "The rest of Annie should be fine."

"'You little idiot.'" Petal echoed the words. "Did Georgia say that out loud, or am I still reading minds, or did I imagine that?"

We all ignored Petal as Annie speed-dialed a number.

"Hello, Pete's Repairs and Auto Wrecking?" she said. "Could you put Mr. Pete on, please?" Annie covered the mouthpiece of the phone with her hand. "That's odd," she said, "another man answered. I always thought Pete worked alone."

Who could blame her? We'd all always thought that.

"Mr. Pete," Annie said a moment later, "could you please come to the parking lot of the Super-Duper Food Ex — well, you know the place. We're having some trouble with the Hummer." Annie paused and we assumed it was because Pete was talking. "No," Annie said, "I don't think it's sabotage this time, or at least I have no proof, but the Hummer is belching dark smoke . . ." Another pause. "Fine. We'll wait for you right here."

Seven of us thought that last little bit was unnecessary. What else were we going to do, leave our only vehicle and a dozen or more bags of groceries behind and walk several miles home? It was hot and it was July, as Rebecca kept reminding us.

"I can't believe," Rebecca said, peeking in to look at the display of the digital clock inside the Hummer, "that we're ten hours and seventeen minutes into July and I still haven't —"

We could only thank the universe that Pete arrived quickly enough to save us from Rebecca going on and on about having to wait so long for her power. Really, Pete arrived so quickly, it practically felt like magic.

"What seems to be the problem, ducks?" Pete said, hopping out of his flatbed pickup truck in all of his blue-jeaned glory.

"We've got a Really Big Shop's worth of groceries to get home before it spoils in this heat," Durinda said.

"And while it may be safe to drive the car in this condition—" Annie started.

"Which I'm sure it's not!" Petal screamed from her position on the ground, arms still over her head.

"—it can't be good for the environment for us to drive a vehicle in this condition," Jackie finished.

"No," Pete said, shaking his head as he studied the smoke-belching Hummer, "I can see that."

"Would you like to know, Mr. Pete," Marcia offered, "how many square inches of shelf space are taken up by a box of Razzle Crunchies?"

"Not at the moment, pet," Pete said, still studying the Hummer. Then he glanced up and caught Marcia's crestfallen look. "Perhaps later on," he suggested. "I'm sure that later on I'd love to hear all about . . . whatever it was you just said."

Pete proceeded to pop the hood on the Hummer and look inside.

"Hmm," he said after a long moment. "I don't think the problem's in here. I think I'll need to look under the beast."

"How do you propose to do that?" Georgia asked. "Do you need me to go back to the house and get the spear for you?"

Georgia was obsessed with the spear that was normally clutched by Daddy Sparky, the suit of armor we dressed up to make it look like Daddy was at home, moving it around from room to room.

"No," Pete said. "I don't think such extreme measures are called for. I'll simply put the old Hummer on cement blocks so I can get a clear view of what is going on."

Pete then disappeared into the back of his pickup, eventually emerging with four very heavy-looking cement blocks, which he laid on the ground in front of the Hummer. The blocks were slanted, so it took us a long time to figure out what Pete was doing. It helped that he told us.

"See," he said, "I'm driving the Hummer up on the blocks, like so, in order to get a better view of the underside of the vehicle."

"I wouldn't do that if I were you," Petal advised from her position on the ground, just barely peeking her head out from under her arms. "You couldn't pay me enough to crawl under a Hummer propped up by a few measly cement blocks."

"It's perfectly fine, pet," Pete said cheerily as he slid beneath the Hummer, "I just slide in like this, get my toolbox out, and—"

It was at that very moment, as Pete positioned himself beneath the Hummer with his tools, his wrench or some other item we couldn't name right then at the ready, that the front wheels of the Hummer slid off their blocks and—

"Oh no!" Petal shrieked. "Mr. Pete is going to get pancaked!"

And *that* moment—that instant, really—as the falling Hummer was bearing down on Pete's startled, raised head, Rebecca impulsively leaped out and grabbed the bumper of the Hummer.

We'd seen the Grinch on TV. We may have been confused sometimes about our religious identity, but we'd seen the Grinch, as all kids everywhere have, and we felt that we were seeing the Grinch again that day as Rebecca grabbed the bumper of the Hummer and lifted the car straight over her head.

"Is this okay now, Mr. Pete?" Rebecca asked with a

rare show of respect. "Am I raising it high enough for you to do the work you need to do?"

"That's fine, pet," Pete said. "That's better than fine. As a matter of fact, it's too fine, so if you can lower the car a bit so I can actually reach what I need to fix . . ."

Rebecca heeded his instructions, lowering the Hummer a few feet so Pete could work on it properly but not letting go of it until Pete was finished and had given her the go-ahead.

When he did, she gently lowered the vehicle and then shifted it a bit so that this time it was resting securely on the blocks.

"Once again," Pete said, "I find myself moved to say that if I hadn't seen this with my own eyes, I'd never have believed it. Do you realize that you saved my life, Rebecca?"

"Oh, I'm sure I didn't . . ." Rebecca started to say in a rare show of modesty.

But just then we realized something. We weren't the only ones to witness Rebecca's superhuman show of strength.

"Did you just get your power?" Pete asked Rebecca. "Is that what happened?"

And just as he spoke, we heard a passerby say, "Did you see what that little girl just did? She saved Pete's life!"

Well, of course everyone in town knew Pete.

Before we knew what was going on, more passersby were stopping to stare, and then a reporter from the local newspaper showed up with a photographer who insisted on taking a picture of Rebecca holding the Hummer over Pete's head.

"What a story!" the reporter said.

"'Little Girl Saves Big Blue-Jeans-Wearing Man's Life!'" the photographer said, envisioning the headline.

"Let's get out of here," Durinda suggested.

"Before worst comes to worst," Georgia said.

"Besides," Zinnia said, "the cats must be eager for their kibble."

"I still can't believe," Pete said, "that Rebecca saved my life. I could have been pancaked!"

"I know," Zinnia said, speaking for a second time and brightening. "Let's go home and read the note that has no doubt been left behind the loose stone in the drawing room for Rebecca. Getting a new note always cheers us all up!"

* * * * * * * *

But when we arrived back at home, Pete in tow, and sped to the drawing room, we didn't find the note we were expecting behind the loose stone.

The note we were expecting should have said something along the lines of:

Rebecca,

Outstanding job getting your power! Thirteen down, three to go.

Of course we were fairly certain that the notes had never used a word as grand as *outstanding* before—we were embellishing—but the notes were typically very encouraging. And after Rebecca's powerful feat—after her *superhuman* feat—we were certainly expecting some encouraging words.

There was just one problem.

The space behind the loose stone was dead empty.

There was no note.

Not to be ominous but . . .

What could this possibly mean?

FIVE

"We should plan a party," Zinnia suggested.

We ignored Zinnia.

"I know what this means," Annie said.

We all waited. And waited.

"Well," Georgia finally said, "do you think you'd like to share your knowledge with us?"

"It simply means," Annie said, "that Rebecca hasn't gotten her power at all."

"I haven't?" Rebecca said, cracking her knuckles. "That's funny. I still feel strong."

"Perhaps you do," Annie said, "but I'm sure if we went out to the Hummer right now you could never lift it."

"I couldn't?" Rebecca said, cracking her knuckles again.

We did wish she would stop that.

"No, of course you couldn't," Annie said. "In times of crisis, people are sometimes capable of incredible feats of strength. But as soon as the crisis is over? The strength is over too."

"Oh, yes," Marcia said eagerly, "I've heard of that. It's like a mother stopping a train or something to save her baby."

"Oh, that's so sweet," Durinda said. "It's like Pete's Rebecca's baby."

Rebecca made a face at this suggestion but Pete didn't look like he minded. Well, there were worse things than being compared to a baby. Like, say, getting pancaked by a Hummer. Pete probably didn't care what anybody said about him right now.

"This is wonderful news!" Marcia said.

"The fact that I don't have my power yet is wonderful news?" Rebecca said.

"Yes," Marcia said. "It means that whoever or whatever leaves those notes for us hasn't lost its knack. You know, odd as it is that some force is so closely attuned to what's going on in this house that it knows the precise moment to leave a new note, it would be even more disturbing if it suddenly stopped. What would it mean if it stopped before we all got our powers and gifts? Would it mean that the note leaver had lost its own power? Would it mean we'd never find out what happened to Mommy and Daddy? In an uncertain universe, those notes are one of the few certain things — why, a note even reached us on a plane! So to have them suddenly stop would mean yet more uncertainty for us."

"Wow, that was a long speech," Georgia said.

"I hate an uncertain universe." Petal shuddered.

"As I say," Rebecca said with another crack of the knuckles, "I'm still feeling fairly strong."

"Okay," Annie said, crossing her arms. "If you're still so strong, prove it."

"Fine," Rebecca said, looking around the drawing room for something to prove it with. At last she settled on the wing chair in front of the fireplace. She bent down, lifted it cleanly off the floor, and then set it back down again.

"That was impressive," Jackie said.

"Oh, come on," Georgia scoffed. "That's not impressive." Georgia went over to the wing chair and bent down to get a firm grip on it. "Why, anyone can . . ." Georgia strained with all her might and after a long moment was only able to lift it a smidgen off the ground before she had to drop it again. "See, anyone can do it."

"Not like Rebecca did it," Marcia observed. "Rebecca did it without showing any sign of effort at all."

"Oh," Rebecca pooh-poohed, "pooh-pooh. Of course Georgia's right. All I did was lift a chair. It's not like lifting a whole Hummer. It was nothing. Now, why don't you all move in for a group hug?"

Rebecca was requesting a group hug? Now, this was

odd. Even odder than the number seven, or Marcia. Still, we thought, as all of us moved toward her, including Pete, maybe after realizing she didn't have her power after all, she simply wanted to express her affection for us.

Once we were in position, all of us encircling Rebecca, we felt our feet gradually leave the earth.

"What's going on?" Petal asked worriedly. "Have I finally worried about something so much that, as Rebecca has warned me many times, I've managed to spin myself right off the planet?"

"I don't know," Georgia's muffled voice said, "that may be the case for you, but I'm fairly certain that the rest of us are being lifted off the ground by Rebecca."

"Who doesn't have her power yet now?" Rebecca said with what can only be described as a maniacal laugh.

"Put us down," Annie commanded. "You may be freakishly strong, but I'm still head of this household."

Rebecca set us down.

"I'm still not impressed," Georgia said. "So she lifted us all off the ground. Big deal. We're just a bunch of little girls. We don't weigh very much. Carl the talking refrigerator is always saying we're too skinny."

"That may be so," Jackie said, "but she lifted Mr. Pete too."

"And Mr. Pete's a big guy," Durinda added. "No offense, Mr. Pete."

"None taken," Pete said. "I am a big guy. And even if no one else is, I'm impressed that Rebecca could lift me, even if I'm not quite as heavy as a Hummer."

"What could this mean?" Marcia was clearly puzzled, and troubled too. "If the crisis of Mr. Pete almost dying gave Rebecca her strength before, why does she still have it? And if this is her power, how is it possible the note leaver hasn't left a note?"

"Who knows?" Rebecca shrugged. "And who cares? Perhaps I've always been freakishly strong but just never knew it."

"We should have a party," Zinnia suggested again. "Having a party is practically like getting a present."

We ignored Zinnia.

"But how could you not have known such a thing about yourself?" Marcia asked.

Rebecca shrugged again. "Maybe it's because I was never tested before. Does anyone want to see if I can still lift the Hummer? After all, the Hummer is still heavier than all of you put together, even when we throw in Mr. Pete."

Seven of us shrugged, and so did Mr. Pete. Might as well go see if she could still lift the Hummer. We weren't exactly sure what that would prove, but we were fairly certain it would prove *something*. Plus, at least two of us were hoping that she couldn't lift it anymore. Bad as a world in which Rebecca could lift all of us at once might be, one in which her strength was so extraordinary she could lift the Hummer whenever she wanted was just too much to think about. It would mean the universe had tilted. It could mean something had happened to the note leaver.

Out we trooped, following Rebecca to the garage.

We'd like to give a big buildup, create an air of suspense here, but there simply wasn't any.

Once we were in the garage, Rebecca lifted the Hummer. Only this time, unlike in the parking lot, where she'd just lifted it by the bumper, she lifted the whole thing clear off the ground, like she was lifting a toothpick.

"Would you all like to climb inside?" Rebecca said. "See if I can still lift it with all of you in it?"

None of us wanted to do that.

Back into the house we trooped.

"I wonder if I'm the strongest girl in the world," Rebecca mused once we were back in the drawing room. "I wonder if I could lift this entire house clean off its foundations . . ."

"Oh brother." Georgia rolled her eyes. "If you're that strong, maybe you should join the circus."

"That's not such a bad idea." Rebecca's eyes gleamed. "I could be the Strong Lady."

"You'd be the Strong Girl, actually," Marcia corrected.

"More like the Strong Idiot," Georgia muttered, but she muttered it very quietly. No doubt, knowing Rebecca's strength, Georgia didn't want to make her angry. Because then who knew what Rebecca might do?

"But I don't think I'm ready for the circus just yet." Rebecca shrugged off the idea. "There's too much I need to do around here first."

"Like what?" Jackie asked.

"Like, I don't know . . ." Rebecca paused, casting her eyes on Petal. Then, with no effort at all, Rebecca picked Petal up in one hand. Petal, who could be something like one of those cute little pill bugs when scared, immediately tucked her knees in and curled herself into a tight ball. That's when Rebecca balanced the curled-up Petal on the very tip of one finger and used her other hand to spin Petal around until she was spinning at an alarming speed.

"Look at me!" Rebecca said. "It's like Petal's a spinning basketball. Maybe I'll join the Harlem Globetrotters!"

"Wait a second," Marcia said. "If this really is Rebecca's power, whether the note leaver knows it or not, then Rambunctious should have her power too."

"That's right, isn't it?" Pete said. "Your cats always get your powers when you do."

Seven Eights plus Pete plus the spinning Petal headed to the cat room, which was like our drawing room, only for cats.

"Phew!" Marcia said when we got there. "It looks like all they're doing is drinking from their water dishes."

Poor Marcia. The way she was worrying about the note leaver, it was almost as bad as Petal worrying about just about anything.

But then one cat—that would be Rambunctious— stopped lapping up water and looked at us. And when Rambunctious saw what Rebecca was doing, she made straight for Precious. A moment later, Precious was curled up and poised on the tip of one of Rambunc-

tious's paws while Rambunctious used a second paw to spin Precious like a basketball.

"Oh no," Marcia said. "Rebecca's cat now has super-human strength too."

"Actually, that would be superkitty strength," Jackie pointed out.

"What can it all mean?" Marcia said.

"I think we should have a party," Zinnia said. "No matter whether Rebecca has found her power or not, no matter what it all means, I think we should have a party—you know, to celebrate Rebecca saving Mr. Pete's life and to celebrate Mr. Pete still being alive."

Fourteen eyes plus Pete's turned to stare at Zinnia.

"What an excellent idea," Annie said. "Why didn't you suggest this sooner?

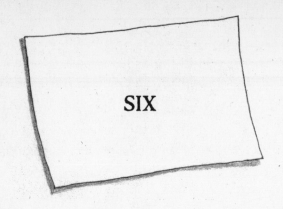

SIX

"So when should we have this party?" Annie asked.

"I suppose it should be on the Fourth of July," Durinda said. "The only problem is, that's so close. I'd need to plan a menu and get special food for the barbecue, particularly since Zinnia says we shouldn't eat meat anymore. I wonder if they sell fillet-of-sole dogs at the supermarket . . ."

"I think having it on the Fourth of July is a lousy idea," Georgia said. "I mean, do we even celebrate the Fourth of July?"

"Isn't that an American holiday?" Petal said. "I always get so confused. Are we in America or are we in Britain?"

We would have liked to laugh in Petal's face over that one. Only problem was, we sometimes got confused ourselves, what with the way we spoke, not to mention the added confusion of the faux British accent

Annie used whenever she wanted to impersonate our model father, Robert Huit.

Hmm . . . we mulled it over.

Well, we supposed, if we did live in the United States, we would feel one way about having a celebration on the Fourth of July. But if we were in England, we were quite certain we would feel an entirely different way about it.

We had studied *some* history.

"Never mind that," Rebecca said, cutting short our mulling. "Since this is to be a celebration of *my* accomplishment" — we did notice how she'd cut Pete right out of the celebration picture — "then I think *I* should get to pick out the day I'm to be celebrated on."

"I hope you're not going to say today," Durinda said, looking horrified. "So much has already happened today. I think it's a bit much to expect me to plan a party and prepare the food all on the same day."

"Plus," Petal said, "I don't much care for going back to do another Really Big Shop right now. Too many scary people tend to gather at the grocery store."

"I think you'll all be pleased with the date I selected," Rebecca said, "and it will give you plenty of time to prepare, much more than if we were to do it on the Fourth."

After a long pause, during which it appeared that

Rebecca was waiting for a drumroll, Jackie prompted, "Are you going to share this information right now or should we go put the groceries away first?"

"We're not going to give you an actual drumroll," Georgia added, "so you might as well get on with it."

But she'd spoken too soon. Because just then, Zinnia picked up a handy pencil and tapped it on the table several times before rapping it smartly on Daddy Sparky as though Daddy Sparky were a giant cymbal.

"That was fun," Zinnia said cheerily. "Would you like me to do it again, Rebecca?"

"That won't be necessary," Rebecca said. "I'm ready to tell you now. The absolute perfect, best ever, fantabuloso day for my celebration is . . . Bastille Day!"

"Bas . . . *what?*" even Marcia felt prompted to say.

"Bastille Day," Rebecca said impatiently. "Weren't any of the rest of you paying attention when we were in France for Uncle George and Aunt Martha's wedding?"

France. Uncle George. Aunt Martha.

We sighed. If only Uncle George and Aunt Martha hadn't left for a three-month-long round-the-world cruise right after their wedding and therefore couldn't be reached, we might have asked Uncle George more about our mother's identical twin and her children. Uncle George did appear to know more about other relatives than our average family member. Too bad he was at sea.

"Why would Bastille Day be the perfect day?" Annie wanted to know. "And when is it anyway?"

"It's celebrated on July fourteenth every year," Rebecca said. "And it's perfect because it's French and we're French. Our last name's Huit, you know, not Ocho or Smith."

"It's all coming back to me now," Marcia said. "Bastille Day . . . Bastille Day . . . doesn't that have something to do with the seventeen hundreds, the French Revolution, the storming of a perfectly horrific prison, and all manner of other awful things?"

"Yes," Rebecca said, "which is why it's also the perfect day to celebrate me."

"Because you're all manner of other awful things?" Petal looked worried. Then she added with a hopeful smile, "Or do you mean you wish you lived in the seventeen hundreds?"

"You had it the first time," Rebecca said. "It's perfect because I am fearsome."

"She means," Jackie whispered to Petal, "that she causes fear, like a fearsome monster. You know, that she's intense and extreme."

"Oh dear," Petal said, and then she fainted.

By the time we revived Petal, we'd decided that we'd had quite enough excitement for one day. We still had thirteen days to plan Rebecca's celebration, so we contented ourselves with doing mundane things like putting the groceries away, seeing Pete off, eating, making great big piles of leaves in Fall and then leaping into them, and going to bed.

As we shut off the lights we did feel as though the day had been incredibly long with so much happening in it. We wondered if there would ever come a day that would feel even longer, maybe even twice as long.

* * * * * * * *

We awoke the next day determined to begin planning Rebecca's celebration. And we might have even made some progress were it not for . . .

"Oh, look," Georgia said, bringing in the morning newspaper and depositing it on Rebecca's plate, "you got your picture on the front page of the newspaper."

Even though the newspaper still got delivered to our house every day, like it did when Mommy and Daddy were here, we almost never bothered to read anything in it. From what we could see, it was mostly filled with world affairs or news about local events, neither of which affected us very much. We couldn't do a thing about the former and had no time for the latter. After all, we had our own set of problems, didn't we?

But on this day, we couldn't ignore the newspaper because . . .

"Little Local Girl Finds Strength of Ten Men!"

That's what the headline above the picture of Rebecca screamed.

The article began, "A little local girl saved a favorite town mechanic yesterday when . . ."

"I'm not sure I like being referred to as 'a little local girl,'" Rebecca said with a sniff.

"At least they didn't call you 'a little loco girl,'" Marcia pointed out.

"I suppose," Rebecca said, "but I was referring to the use of *little*. Anyway, other than that, this is a smashing piece on me. I think it—"

"Smashing?" Annie cut her off. "How can you possibly think this is smashing, unless you mean *smash* in a bad way, as in 'destroy'? Why, this is the worst thing to happen to us since Mommy and Daddy disappeared!"

"Or died," Georgia added for Rebecca, who was too busy admiring her picture in the newspaper to say it.

"How can you possibly say that?" Rebecca demanded of Annie. "Look at me: I'm famous."

"Which is exactly my—" Annie started to say, but she couldn't finish because it was then that the phone began to ring.

It was then that people began knocking at our door, and some of them began pounding.

After six months and one day of trying to fly under the radar, of trying to keep the outside world from realizing that eight little girls were living home alone, the world had found its way to our doorstep.

And it was all Rebecca's fault.

Or the fault of her power.

Her power that the note leaver seemed unaware of.

* * * * * * * *

Of the two—the perpetually ringing phone and the eternally pounding door—the phone was the easier to ignore. We rarely ever bothered answering the phone during normal times, or what passed for normal in our world, because a ringing phone hardly ever meant anything good or useful for us. We preferred to let the machine take our calls, so really all this meant was more ringing to ignore, and we quickly solved that problem by turning off the ringer.

But people pounding on our door was a different matter. After all, we did need to go outside to send and get the mail, so that we could pay the bills on time and see if we'd received any more invitations; we could count on the carrier pigeons that visited us occasionally to bring irregular mail but never regular mail. Plus, we did just plain need to go outside. How would we find our parents if we could never leave the house again? We were fairly certain we'd never find them *in* the house. And, too, we needed the normalcy of lying in a hammock and staring at clouds.

But we couldn't do any of that with a passel of reporters parked outside our door. We couldn't do any of that if each time we opened the door, photographers snapped pictures, videographers ran video cameras, and reporters kept trying to shove their microphones into the gap, always asking the same questions: "Can we speak to the little local girl about her extraordinary feat of strength?" "Can we speak to the little local girl's parents about what it feels like to raise such a temporarily strong daughter?" "Has the little local girl's strength gone back to normal yet or can she still lift a Hummer?"

"It's not my fault, it's not my fault," Rebecca asserted for the fiftieth time when one of us said for the fiftieth time that Rebecca was to blame for our new-found lack of privacy.

"No one said you were to blame," Annie said.

Rebecca crossed her arms and harrumphed. "No one except Georgia and Petal, and occasionally you." Rebecca added another harrumph.

"People just resent all the attention and the loss of privacy," Jackie pointed out. "But no one really blames you."

"Could have fooled me," Rebecca said. "What would you all have had me do? *Not* use my strength and instead let Pete get pancaked?"

We shuddered at that. None of us would have wanted Pete gone from the world. The world was too scary by half as it was.

"It's July second," Marcia said, "just one day after Rebecca got her power. Maybe the note leaver simply had to go away for a day or take the day off for some reason. Maybe it's there now. I think I'll go check."

"I'll come too," Zinnia said. "I always like checking for the notes."

But a moment later they came running back, sadly noteless, as we all tried to discover the source of the greatest pounding yet. Most people run from danger, but the circumstances of our lives often caused us to run toward it.

At last we located the source of the pounding: the kitchen window.

"Mr. Pete," Durinda said, throwing open the window, "what are you doing out there pounding on our window?"

Pete vaulted over the sill and into the house, or he vaulted as well as a man of his size could vault. Then he reached back out and down and pulled in Mrs. Pete. And then he pulled in two suitcases after him. Then, finally, he pulled in his cat, Old Felix.

"What are you doing?" Durinda asked again.

Not that any of us minded their coming for what looked like a longer-than-usual visit, but we were curious.

"I saw the article in the paper," Pete said, "and figured right away that reporters would start hounding you and that with all the extra attention focused on your house, it would be no time before some nosy parker realized there were no adults living here and then the jig would be up."

"So we decided to come and pretend to be your

uncle and aunt again," Mrs. Pete said, "so that the world would believe you're being supervised adultly."

"I don't think *adultly* is an actual word," Marcia felt compelled to point out.

We ignored her.

"How long do you plan to stay?" Rebecca asked.

"For the duration," Pete said, "or for as long as you need us."

SEVEN

Pete took care of those pesky nosy-parker reporters in no time.

Opening the front door bravely and standing firm there more bravely still, he announced, "This is private property. If you don't get off it this instant, I shall call the police and have you all taken to the hoosegow."

"So?" one particularly pesky reporter said. "Then we'll just go stand in the street and shout our questions and snap our pictures from there."

Oh no. Would we never enjoy the luxury of being private citizens again? What had Rebecca gotten us into?

"Yes," Pete said, "I suppose you can do that for about an hour or two, but I'll just build a fence so high, you'll never be able to climb over it."

"Well, then we could—" the particularly pesky reporter started to say, but Pete cut him off.

"I know, I know," Pete said with a weary sigh, "you'll

get a helicopter and a telephoto lens and fly overhead. Well, just try it. I am very good with a slingshot, plus I think you'll find if you check with public records that this house is under a no-fly zone."

All of the reporters, the regularly pesky and the particularly pesky, dispersed with grumbles.

"Is that true, Mr. Pete," Petal asked, "that our house is under that thing you said? I rather like to think of us living beneath one giant protective bubble."

"Of course it's not true," Georgia said meanly to Petal. Then she turned to Pete. "Is it?"

"'Fraid not," Pete admitted. "At least, not yet. But I know a man who knows a man who works in public records, so I'll tell the man I know to tell the man he knows to put a note in your file to that effect."

Pete always seemed to know a man who knew a man who. He was very handy that way.

"Now I'll just go get that impenetrable fence built," Pete said. "Shouldn't take more than an hour or six. Oh, and Rebecca?"

"Yes?"

"Don't feel bad about all this mess with the reporters and such. It's not really your fault."

"Of course I don't feel bad," Rebecca said. "I saved your life, didn't I?"

"Yes, you did. Why is it that I think you'll constantly be reminding me of that fact?"

* * * * * * * *

One or six hours later, when Pete had finished erecting our impenetrable fence, we got down to more important business.

"If we're going to have a party in just twelve days," Durinda said, "we really do need to start making a guest list."

"I'll get a piece of paper and a pen," Jackie offered, and she did.

"So who shall we put on the list?" Annie said, pen poised as she sat at the dining-room table, the Petes and the rest of us gathered around.

"Well, I think we should invite all of us," Petal said, "meaning us Eights."

Most of us chose to ignore that, except for:

Marcia, who said, "I don't think Annie needs to write all our names down. I should think we'd remember us."

And Georgia, who said, "Can't we leave Rebecca's name off?"

And Rebecca, who said, "It's my celebration and I resent that remark, even if I do sort of resemble it."

"I don't know what that means," Petal said.

"That's okay," Jackie said. "I don't think any of us is supposed to."

"We should put the Petes down," Petal said, "Mr. and Mrs."

"That hardly seems necessary," Annie pointed out, "since they're already here. I think we'll be able to remember them too."

"Then what's the point in even making a list?" Zinnia said, looking crestfallen. "Why make a list if everyone who is going to be invited and who is therefore likely to come is already here?"

"I don't know." Durinda shrugged. "I only know that it's the thing to do. You know, from watching Mommy do it. You want to have a party," Durinda said with another shrug, "you have to make lists."

"I was thinking maybe we should invite a few other people to my celebration," Rebecca said, "maybe liven things up."

"But who else is there to invite?" Marcia said. "All of the most important people, except for Mommy and Daddy, are already on the list. Or they would be if Annie would only write their names down."

"What about Will Simms?" Zinnia suggested. "We could invite Will Simms. We all like Will Simms."

This was true. All summer long, since school had ended, we'd been wanting to invite him over to play but hadn't felt that we were able to. There's a lot you can do when you're eight little girls living home alone. You can run the household. You can acquire powers and gifts. You can try to solve the mysteries of the universe. But one thing you can't do, unless you are very careful about it, is invite friends over, because if their parents discover there is no adult supervision, objections might be raised. But now we had adult supervision, in the form of the Petes.

"Put Will's name down!" Durinda said.

"Put Will's name down!" Jackie said.

"Put Will's name down!" Georgia said.

"Put Will's name down!" Marcia said.

"Not a bad idea," Rebecca said, "even if I didn't think of it myself."

Petal didn't say anything. She just spun in a happy tizzy, daydreaming of Will.

"Put Will's name down!" Zinnia said, even though she'd already suggested him once.

"All right, all right," Annie said. "No need to shout at me. Didn't you see me put it down just as soon as Zinnia suggested it?"

Mrs. Pete looked at us all closely. "Do you all have a . . . *crush* on this Will Simms?"

Sixteen cheeks blushed crimson. Eight heads shook violently.

We refused to respond any further to that remark.

"What about Mandy Stenko?" Zinnia suggested. "If

we invite one classmate, I suppose we should invite the other classmate."

There was somewhat less enthusiasm for this suggestion than there had been for Zinnia's last one, but eventually we agreed that Annie should add Mandy's name to the list. Mandy had been much better of late, and anyway, she was really no competition for us in terms of Will's affections.

Not that we were competing over him or anything.

"These are both fine suggestions, I suppose," Rebecca said, "but I was thinking of inviting someone a little more . . . *dangerous*."

"We could invite the McG and the Mr. McG," Zinnia suggested. "They could be dangerous, in that they might bring a homework assignment with them."

Zinnia had instantly become our expert on making up guest lists. Well, she was our party girl.

"That's not who—" Rebecca started, but Annie cut her off.

"Yes, I think I will add their names," Annie said. "Perhaps if we invite them to a party in the summer, they'll take it easy on us in the fall."

Georgia snorted at this.

"Fine," Rebecca said, "you can invite them to my party, but I still think we should invite a few more . . . *dangerous* people to liven things up."

"Like who?" Jackie asked mildly.

"Like the Wicket," Rebecca said.

Seven jaws, plus Pete's and Mrs. Pete's, dropped.

"Like Frank Freud," Rebecca said, "just as soon as I can locate where he's living now."

Seven mouths, plus Pete's and Mrs. Pete's, snapped shut.

And then everyone except Rebecca began to splutter.

"But we can't do that!"

"That would be insanity!"

"That would be *death!*" Guess who on that one?

"Yes, we can do that," Rebecca said, "no, it wouldn't be insanity, and no, it wouldn't be death. What it would be is smart."

"Smart?" those of us who weren't scared out of our wits shouted.

"Yes, smart," Rebecca said. "Keep your friends close and your enemies closer."

Pete let out a low whistle.

Rebecca was busy being smug over her pronouncement, so it took her a moment to ask, "Why'd you just whistle like that, Mr. Pete?"

"Because of you, pet," he said simply. "Why, you're turning into a regular Machiavelli right before our very eyes."

"Machia-who?" Rebecca asked with a sneer, though she usually tried not to sneer around Pete since even she recognized that we did often need him.

"I guess you haven't studied him in school yet," Pete said. "But one day you will. And when you do, Rebecca, I doubt anything he said will come as any great surprise to you."

"Machiavelli," Marcia informed us. "Italian guy. Dead for hundreds of years. Lots of tough ideas about how things should work. You pronounce the *ch* like *k*."

Hmm . . . except for the Italian and the dead-for-hundreds-of-years parts, he did sound just like Rebecca.

"Anyway," Rebecca said, "if the Wicket or Frank Freud get out of line, with my new strength that may or may not be my power, I can toss them."

* * * * * * * *

Drawing up a guest list had taken a lot out of us and we were eager for some liquid refreshment.

"Annie and Marcia didn't think to get any mango juice," Durinda said, "nor did they get any juice boxes, so I guess I'll just squeeze us some fresh orange juice. Jackie?"

Jackie followed Durinda into the kitchen as usual, leaving some of us to wonder: Jackie was always so agreeable about helping out, but what if one day she mutinied or tried to stage a coup, like the time Marcia tried to take the reins of the household from Annie?

But no, we thought. Mutiny wasn't Jackie's style and she was certainly no Marcia, obsessed with power. She was simply Jackie, the only one among us without any serious issues, and we were grateful for her being the way she was.

"Fresh-squeezed juice is ready!" Durinda called, bringing in a tray with a pitcher full of juice and some glasses.

If Jackie was our normal one, we did worry about Durinda sometimes. We worried that one day she'd hunt down a string of pearls and a frilly apron and never take either off again. It was a bit scary sometimes, Durinda's kitchen self.

"What's this?" Rebecca said, peering into a glass once Durinda had finished pouring.

"It's juice," Durinda said, stating the obvious, "from fresh-squeezed oranges. I squeezed them myself."

"If it's fresh-squeezed," Rebecca said, "then there should be pulp."

"There isn't any," Durinda said. "I strained it. No kid likes pulp."

"You didn't throw out the pulp, did you?" Rebecca demanded.

"No, she didn't," Jackie said. Then she disappeared

into the kitchen, returning a moment later with a glass measuring cup filled with awful, disgusting pulp.

Rebecca took the glass measuring cup, raised it to her lips, and drained it dry.

"Ah, pulp," Rebecca said, wiping her lips with the back of her hand. "We strong girls like drinking the pulp."

Some of us were beginning to think that Rebecca's power, if it was her power, was going to her head.

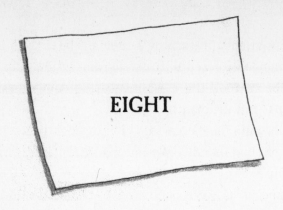

EIGHT

"Have we got any more pulp in the house?" Rebecca said, sweating as she came indoors from outside, where she'd been doing something in the newly fenced-in front yard with Petal. We craned our necks around Rebecca, who was standing in the doorway. There was poor Petal behind her, spread-eagled on the lawn. We wondered what they'd been up to. We wondered if Petal was still alive.

"I *said*," Rebecca said testily, "have we got any more pulp in the house?"

"How should I know?" Durinda said just as testily. "I'm not your maid. Besides, it's a holiday. Why don't you go see for yourself?"

We assumed Durinda meant for her to go see if there was any more pulp in the house and not for Rebecca to go see if it was a holiday. We already knew it was a holiday, since it was in fact the Fourth of July, which we were only half celebrating since we still hadn't decided where we geographically stood on the issue.

"I'll bet if I were Zinnia and I asked for pulp, you'd get it for me in a second," Rebecca grumbled.

"Yes, I would," Durinda grumbled back, "but that's because Zinnia is sweet while you're . . ."

"Yes, I do know exactly what I am," Rebecca said, filling the void left by Durinda's unfinished sentence.

"Just for the record," Zinnia piped up, "I'd never ask for a glass of pulp."

"We all know that," Annie said.

"And if I did go crazy and ask for one," Zinnia went on, "I'd still have enough sanity left to also say *please* and *thank you*. Those are, after all, the magic words."

"We know that too," Annie said.

"You people make me crazier than I already am," Rebecca said, trudging off to the kitchen.

"I hope Petal's still alive," Jackie said.

"Do you see the way her little chest is heaving up and down?" Marcia observed. "I think that means she must be."

"Phew," Georgia said, "that's a relief."

We all turned to Georgia. When had she ever cared about Petal?

"What?" Georgia stared back at us, surprised and offended. "Where would I be without Petal? Why, without Petal, there'd be no one for me to call 'you little idiot.' I'd be devastated."

Of course.

Rebecca came back from the kitchen, wiping her mouth with the back of her hand. A glass of raw eggs, a glass of pulp, a glass of orange-tinted battery acid — really, at this point it was anyone's guess what she'd been drinking in there.

"Well, I'm off again," she announced heartily. Then she paused, considering. "I wonder if Petal's up to continuing now . . ."

"That's nice of you to worry about Petal for once —" Annie started.

"Well, I wouldn't go so far as to say I'm *worrying* about her," Rebecca corrected, "just wondering."

"Whatever the verb," Annie said, "I am curious: just what are you doing with — or perhaps I should say *to* — Petal out there?"

Rebecca shrugged. "If you're so curious, why don't you come watch? It's a free country, after all. Isn't that what this day is all about?"

* * * * * * * *

We all, including the Petes, followed Rebecca out to the front yard.

"Are you ready for more?" Rebecca asked Petal, grabbing Petal's hands and pulling her to her feet.

"I don't think —" Petal started to say, but Rebecca

just tossed Petal over her shoulder and began racing around the house with her.

"That's what you call the fireman's carry," Rebecca informed us after a few laps. "Come on now, Petal, position yourself for the piggyback."

"I don't think—" Petal started to say.

Before we knew it, Rebecca was racing around the house some more with Petal clinging to her back for dear life. We knew then where the term *piggyback* had originally come from, because poor Petal was squealing like a pig.

"Okay," Rebecca said when she'd finished a few laps of that version. "Now, Petal, remember how to do Estonian style?"

Estonian style? What was going on here?

"I don't think—" Petal started to say.

In a moment, Petal was hanging upside down on Rebecca's back, her legs around Rebecca's shoulders, her hands holding on to Rebecca's waist.

More racing around the house ensued.

We had no idea what was happening, but in a way it was fun, kind of like watching some bizarre sporting event. It wasn't exactly like fireworks at dusk at the beach, but something felt celebratory about it. Perhaps because it was different.

We liked different.

Well, except for Petal, who'd never really liked different and certainly wasn't liking it any better right now.

"This is all very entertaining," Annie said when
Rebecca had ceased her racing once more. "Well, probably
not for Petal," she added. "But might it be possible for one
to ask just what exactly are you supposed to be doing?"

But Rebecca ignored her and turned to Pete.

"Do you still have those cement blocks you used to
prop the Hummer up?" she asked him.

Pete nodded.

"Can you bring them out here and set them up on
the lawn?"

"I suppose I can do that," Pete said thoughtfully,
"but what—"

"You only need two," Rebecca said, cutting him off,

"not all four. The requirement is only two dry obstacles."

Dry obstacles?

"Now," Rebecca said, "who wants to go pull out that old wading pool we used to use when we were smaller?"

"I do! I do!" Zinnia cried, raising her hand.

"Very well," Rebecca said, accepting the offer.

"Oh, good," Zinnia said cheerily, trotting off to get the pool. Halfway across the lawn, she stopped, turned around to us, and shouted, "I have no idea why I'm doing this or what it all means, but this is fun!" And then she continued with her trotting.

Soon Pete had two cement blocks set up on the lawn, and Zinnia had hauled out the old wading pool. At the end Jackie had had to help her pull it the rest of the way across the yard. We doubted it weighed as much as the twenty-five-pound bag of kibble Zinnia had lifted at the grocery store three days ago, but it was awkward in size, being large enough to hold eight of us when we were little.

Or littler.

Rebecca got out the hose and began filling the wading pool.

It did take a bit of time.

"There," she said when she was done, pleased. "So, do you think that's about a meter deep?"

"A meter deep?" Marcia said in a rare scoffing tone. "A meter is similar in length to a yard. I doubt you have even six inches, also known as half a foot or one-sixth of a yard, in that thing."

"Oh, well." Rebecca shrugged. "Nothing's ever perfect, is it? Still, it's only practice right now. It'll just have to do as the water obstacle."

Dry obstacles? Water obstacle?

But before any of us could ask a question out loud, as opposed to in our heads, Rebecca was off racing around the dry obstacles and running through the water obstacle. She was racing with Petal hanging upside down on her back in what we now recognized to be the Estonian style.

We still had no idea what we were looking at, but at least we were becoming comfortable with the terminology.

"I'm just glad," Georgia said, "that Mr. Pete erected that impenetrable fence."

"Georgia's right," Annie said.

Georgia's right? Those were words almost as rare in our experience as *Rebecca's right* or *Petal's right.*

"I am?" Georgia asked, as surprised as anyone.

"Yes, of course," Annie said. "We have enough problems in our lives without having reporters or neighbors or strangers seeing this." She indicated with her hand the Petal-carrying Rebecca as Rebecca raced through the wading pool again and serpentined once more around the cement blocks. "Whatever . . . *this* is," Annie added.

"Yes," Georgia said with some degree of pride, "that was right of me to come up with that." Then she frowned. "Although I'm not sure that's what I meant."

We might have questioned Georgia as to just what she had meant, but Rebecca stopped her racing then, dropping Petal at our feet.

Mrs. Pete immediately went to Petal. It was handy to have her around for things like that because it meant Durinda and Jackie were free to circle Rebecca with the rest of us as we tried to figure out just what had been going on.

"So that's it then," Rebecca said, slightly out of breath. "I do wish I had Jackie's speed — you know, to make the racing part easier on my legs and lungs — but with my strength it's mostly just a breeze." She turned to Annie. "I'll need about fifteen hundred dollars from the checkbook. No, better make that two thousand dollars, just to be on the safe side."

"Two thousand dollars?" Annie looked aghast. "Whatever for?"

Rebecca looked aghast at Annie's aghastment. "Why, for the Finnish Wife-Carrying Championship, of course."

"The Finn —" Annie started to say, but Marcia cut her off.

"Oh, I know all about that!" Marcia said excitedly.

"I read about it somewhere once." Then her expression grew puzzled. "But why didn't I recognize that from what Rebecca was doing with Petal?" And then her expression eased. "Maybe it's because of the way Rebecca was doing it — you know, the reduced size of the water obstacle and all that."

"Okay," Annie said, "I can understand why Marcia might know about this . . . Finnish Wife-Carrying thing. Marcia just seems to know lots of bizarre little facts. But how do *you* know about it, Rebecca?"

"Because I read about it on Mommy's computer, didn't I?" Rebecca said boldly.

We reeled back from her. Mommy's computer was in Mommy's private study. We almost never went in there; we rarely used her computer the few times we did go in there; and none of us ever went in there alone.

"So what?" Rebecca dared us. "That night I was doing chin-ups on the chandelier and all those other exercises, I got bored and needed a break. So I went in Mommy's private study and began looking through those files we'd looked at that one time. And when I got bored with that, I began surfing the Internet. That's when I learned about the Finnish Wife-Carrying Championship. And that is why I now need two thousand dollars. So Petal and I can go to Finland and compete. I'm sure we can win this year."

Even though Petal was already lying on the ground, she still managed to faint at this.

Mrs. Pete immediately began fanning Petal, and soon Petal was revived. We weren't sure if Petal was happy about this.

"But Petal's not your *wife!*" Georgia objected.

"So?" There was Rebecca's shrug again. "Not everyone carries his own wife in a Finnish Wife-Carrying Championship. If your wife's too heavy, you're allowed to borrow your neighbor's wife, or even search for a wife farther afield if need be. I'm confident that over time Petal and I can beat the record set by Margo Uosong of Estonia."

"Who is Margo Uosong?" Jackie wondered.

"Only the person who holds the record of having won five Wife-Carrying Championships," Rebecca said, "that's who."

My, it sounded like Rebecca had done her research for once.

"Give us enough years competing," Rebecca went on, "I'm sure we can top that."

"I don't think so," Marcia said thoughtfully.

"How can you say that?" Rebecca said. "Did you not see the ease with which we negotiated the two dry obstacles and the one water obstacle? I'm sure we'd have the fastest time."

"Maybe so," Marcia agreed, "but you still can't compete."

"You mean outside of the fact that I would never give Rebecca two thousand dollars to do this crazy thing?" Annie said.

"Yes," Marcia said, "even outside of that. You see," she said, turning to Rebecca, "you'd be immediately disqualified."

"I'd be *what?*" Rebecca was outraged. And given her newfound strength, that was a scary thing to see.

"Petal certainly would," Marcia said calmly. "I'm familiar with the rules set forth by the International Wife-Carrying Competition Rules Committee, and in addition to the rules about length of the obstacle course and the rules about which wives are available and all that other stuff, it gives a minimum age for the wife. It doesn't say anything about the age of the wife-carrier, but the wife has to be over seventeen years of age."

Apparently, Rebecca hadn't done her research quite thoroughly enough.

"But that's insane!" Rebecca objected. "You mean I have to wait more than nine years to compete? But I'm ready now!"

"That may be the case," Marcia said. "But there's another rule that disqualifies you."

"And that is?" Rebecca demanded, scowling furiously.

"The rules clearly state," Marcia said, "and I quote, 'All participants must have fun.'" Marcia paused, cast a meaningful look at the supine Petal. "Look at Petal. Does Petal look like she's having fun?"

We looked. We had to admit, she did not.

"So you see—" Marcia started, but Rebecca cut her off.

"Fine," Rebecca said with a huff. Then she reached down, scooped Petal off the ground, and threw her over her shoulder in what we now recognized as the fireman's carry.

"Excuse me? Rebecca?" Petal poked Rebecca in the shoulder. "What are you doing?"

"Why, we need to practice some more, of course," Rebecca said.

"Practice?" Petal echoed. "But I thought Marcia just disqualified me."

"We still have to practice," Rebecca said, "so we'll be ready in a little over nine years' time to compete. I'll bet we could really be ready after nine years of practice."

"I don't think—" Petal said.

"And who knows?" Rebecca said. "After nine years of practice, you'll come to think of this as fun, meeting that requirement too."

"I don't think—" Petal said.

"Oh, and in nine years' time," Rebecca said, turning to Annie, "if you're still not willing to give me two thousand dollars to take Petal to Finland with me, I'll start a lemonade stand and raise the money myself."

And then she was off again, racing poor Petal around the yard. A moment later Rambunctious burst through the cat door—which was like our door, only for cats— with Precious slung over her shoulder in the fireman's carry, and she began racing around the lawn too.

"Does anyone mind if I go for a swim in the old wading pool?" Zinnia asked.

We ignored her.

"Well, that was fun," Durinda said, brushing her hands together in a so-much-for-that motion.

"Yes," Georgia agreed, "just another nutty day in our nutty family."

"I hope Petal will be okay," Jackie said as Rebecca whizzed by with Petal again. "She's been hanging upside down for so long, all the blood's rushed to her head."

"She does look like a terrified tomato attached to a body," Marcia observed.

"I can't believe Rebecca thought I'd just give her two thousand dollars so she could take Petal to Finland," Annie said. "The gall of that girl!"

"Where'd I leave my toolbox, Jill?" Pete asked Mrs. Pete.

"Where you always do, dear," Mrs. Pete said. "Why?"

"I need to take down that fence," Pete said.

"But why?" Jackie said. "I thought you put it up there to protect us from reporters and the like."

"I did," Pete agreed. "But Rebecca's incident with the Hummer was three days ago. Reporters have short attention spans, so they should be on to something else and we should be safe from them now. Besides . . ." He paused, looking uncertain as to whether or not it was wise to finish his thought.

"Besides what?" Jackie prompted.

"With the fence up," Pete said, "people may not be able to see us, and that is a good thing. But with it up, we also can't see out. And I think we need to—you know, if something evil this way comes."

"You're getting rid of the fence?" Petal shrieked as Rebecca raced by with her once more. "I certainly hope you don't cancel the no-fly zone!"

NINE

"Jackie," Rebecca instructed, "get out the bouncy boots and put them in the front yard."

"Aye, aye," Jackie said, saluting smartly.

"Zinnia," Rebecca instructed, "get out the wall-walkers and put them in the front yard."

"Aye, aye," Zinnia said, trying to salute in the manner Jackie had but succeeding only in poking herself in the eye.

"Annie," Rebecca started to instruct.

"Don't instruct me," Annie said. "You're not the boss of me."

"You're not the boss of me either," Durinda said, heading off to the kitchen.

"I think I'll help Durinda since Jackie's busy with the bouncy boots," Georgia said. Then, as she was nearly out the door, she mumbled, "No one's the boss of me."

We knew why she only mumbled it. Georgia was

scared Rebecca would replace Petal with her for the Finnish Wife-Carrying.

"I'm curious," Marcia said to Rebecca, "why are you having the others bring the bouncy boots and the wall-walkers into the front yard?"

"Well," Rebecca said, "we can't very well have a party without some sort of entertainment for our guests, can we?"

Yes, it was finally July 14—Bastille Day!—and we were getting ready for our big party. We'd sent out invitations and, surprisingly, all the invitees had RSVPed yes. Most of us were scared of some of those invitees who had said yes, but we were grateful that at least they had the good manners to RSVP. It was our experience that some people could be rather lax in that department.

Just that morning we'd gone to the really big supermarket, the one whose name we'd name if only it weren't so long, in order to get enough food and party goods. Durinda had been pleased to see they were having a big sale on red-white-and-blue party goods—"Eighty percent off," she'd said, "we're practically stealing these!"—since what hadn't sold on the Fourth of July could easily be used for a Bastille Day celebration. The party was set to start at 1:00 p.m., and now here was Rebecca telling us we needed some sort of entertainment for our guests.

Okay, maybe she was ordering us around.

"Could I go get the little pink car?" Petal piped up. "I think some of our guests would find it very entertainment-y to ride around the front lawn in the little pink car."

The little pink car was one of Mommy's inventions, as were the bouncy boots and the wall-walkers. Mommy was such a great scientist-inventor. We sighed. We did miss Mommy, and Daddy too.

"You're probably the only one who'd want to do that," Rebecca said to Petal. "But go ahead. I suppose we need to find some way to keep you happily entertained since I'll be too busy being the center of attention to do any wife-carrying of you today."

* * * * * * * *

Mandy Stenko was the first to arrive . . .

. . . at 12:45 p.m.

"Have I missed anything?" she asked excitedly as soon as her mother had dropped her off and she'd waved goodbye.

"I don't think that's possible," Rebecca said, "since the party isn't supposed to start for another fifteen minutes."

"Actually," Marcia said, consulting her watch, "make that fourteen minutes. A whole minute has passed since Mrs. Stenko dropped Mandy off."

We ignored Marcia. Funny how that was getting easier to do.

"Haven't you ever heard of being fashionably late?" Georgia asked Mandy.

"Oh dear." Mandy covered her mouth with her hand. "Have I made another social faux pas?"

"Just because it's Bastille Day," Rebecca said, "there's no reason to start speaking French. No one will understand you."

"I think," Mandy said, "since there are fourteen minutes left until the party starts—"

"Actually, that's twelve minutes now," Marcia interrupted after another consult with her watch.

"I'll just go see if anyone needs help in the kitchen until that time, whenever it is," Mandy said, and she scampered off.

"Wow," Annie said to Rebecca, "the party hasn't even started yet and already you're making our guests feel welcome."

* * * * * * * *

Eleven minutes later, at exactly 1:00 p.m., Will Simms was dropped off by his mother. We liked a person who knew to arrive exactly on time for a party.

Okay, maybe we just really liked Will Simms.

"What time shall I come back for Will?" Mrs. Simms yelled out the window to us.

"When the party's over!" Rebecca yelled back.

"Sounds perfect," Mrs. Simms said with a happy wave, and she drove off.

We really liked Mrs. Simms too.

Mandy and the others working in the kitchen must have heard the yelling because a moment later everyone was out on the lawn, all gathered around Will.

"It's so good to see you, Will," Mandy said, batting her eyelashes at him.

"Do you have something in your eye, Mandy?" Jackie asked, concerned.

"I've got a pointy stick I could use to get it out," Georgia offered.

"It's good to see everyone too," Will said as Mandy drew back sharply from Georgia. "I've been dying to hear what you all have been up to this summer."

"I went to Antarctica," Mandy said, "and mastered tensies at jacks."

"Wow," Will said, "that's, um, impressive. But what about you, Eights?"

So naturally we told him all about Uncle George and Aunt Martha's wedding, going to France, Petal spending most of the month of June under various beds, the new details about our family that we'd learned in France, and the saving of Rebecca at the top of the Eiffel Tower.

"In French that's called La Tour Eiffel," Mandy said.

We ignored her.

"I was so scared the whole month," Petal said, looking ashamed of herself for once. "That's why I spent all that time under the bed."

"That's okay," Will said, putting a hand on her shoulder. "Bravery isn't never being scared. Bravery is doing the thing that needs to be done even when you are scared. And you came through for Rebecca when you needed to, right?"

Petal straightened her spine and suddenly looked very proud of herself, taller even.

Do you see why we loved Will Simms so much?

"And how about you, Rebecca?" Will asked. "We're nearly halfway through July. Have you received your power yet?"

At the mention of Rebecca's power, Petal grew smaller again. We could tell what she was thinking. Before the party we'd discussed that with the guests we had coming, it would be unwise of Rebecca to show off her freakish strength. But who ever knew with Rebecca? She could forget at any moment and begin racing Petal through dry and water obstacles again.

"I think I'll go ride the little pink car for a bit," Petal piped up in a nervously cheerful voice. "Bye!"

And off went Petal to get in her car.

"About my power," Rebecca said. "I think the answer is yes and no."

"How is that possible?" Will asked.

But before anyone could explain, the next guest arrived:

Frank Freud.

It was July and the midday temperature was well over ninety degrees. Why was he wearing a suit and tie? And was that sweat pouring off his egghead?

"I'm not sure exactly what I'm doing here," he said nervously.

"You're here because I invited you," Rebecca said. "I'm keeping my friends close and my enemies closer." Then she linked her arm through his. "How's this? Are you feeling closer now?"

"Very," he said, his head sweating even more. "In fact, I think the word I'm looking for is *too*."

"Too closer?" Marcia said, puzzled. "But that's not grammatically correct."

"And you call yourself a former educator," Georgia scoffed.

"Look," Zinnia said, pointing to where all the cats were gathered, having their own Bastille Day celebration. "As soon as Frank Freud showed up, all their hairs stood on end, even Old Felix's. I wonder what it means. Perhaps I should ask them?"

"Here," Rebecca said, leading Frank Freud to the wall-walkers. "Your feet are surprisingly small for a grown man's. I think these should fit you."

"But what am I supposed to do with them?" he asked, taking off his shoes and slipping his feet into the wall-walkers.

"They're wall-walkers," Rebecca said, as though the answer should be obvious. "You walk up and down walls with them. You walk across the ceiling if a ceiling is available."

"Oh, I see," he said, gazing up at the side of our big stone house, practically a mansion. "Very well then . . ."

He began walking up the wall as Petal drove by with a zippy beep of her horn.

"Those wall-walkers look like fun," Mandy said wistfully. "Could I try that next?"

"I'm not sure there'll be a next," Rebecca said. "It's probably best we just keep him busy. Besides, this isn't a carnival with rides."

"I know," Jackie offered, "Mandy could use the bouncy boots!"

"What are those?" Mandy asked, looking skeptical.

Rather than answering, Durinda got the boots and helped Mandy into them.

"Now what do I do?" Mandy asked.

"Why, you bounce," Annie said.

"What else would a person do with bouncy boots?" Georgia added.

Mandy jumped just the tiniest bit off the ground, setting off a series of small bounces.

"You can bounce harder than that," Zinnia encouraged her. "The nice thing about bouncing outdoors is that you never have to worry about hitting your head on the ceiling."

"Just be sure to stay away from tree branches," Marcia warned as Mandy began bouncing ever higher and higher.

"Oh my!" Mandy shouted down to us as her bouncing soared her well above the roof of our house. "This is shockingly enjoyable!"

"I see this party's going pretty much as one would expect a party thrown by the Eights to go."

Wait a second? Who just said that?

We turned to see the McG and the Mr. McG standing there.

They were wearing shorts and T-shirts, and, as they had been when they were spotted thirteen days earlier, they were once again holding hands!

"What are you two," Georgia said with disgust, "on a second honeymoon?"

"Pretty much," the Mr. McG said. "Ever since she became Principal McG. I love a powerful woman who bears my name."

"Blech," Georgia said, which was not exactly good party-hosting manners but we did understand.

"Can I offer you some refreshments?" Durinda offered, no doubt to make up for Georgia's rudeness. Also because she was Durinda.

"What do you have?" the McG asked.

Oops! We'd been so excited to see our friends from school, we'd forgotten to bring out the food and drinks!

Quickly, we all did our best to rectify that problem. Soon, the long party table that Pete had brought out earlier in the day and that Mrs. Pete had put a red-white-and-blue paper tablecloth over was covered with a punch bowl, cups, and serving dishes with various salads: fruit, potato, three-bean, egg. Not all mixed together, of course.

It did seem like an awful lot of salads and not enough other stuff, but we'd heard this was the type of food people served at outdoor parties in the summer. We'd read all about it in a magazine on entertaining.

"We have this lovely mango punch," Durinda offered.

"Did you save me a glass of pulp?" Rebecca asked, cracking her knuckles and scratching her belly.

Oh, Rebecca.

But before Durinda could serve any punch, a cab pulled up. Who could possibly be arriving in a cab?

A moment later, our next-door neighbor the Wicket popped out, and we smelled the increasing aroma of fruitcake as the human toadstool cautiously approached us.

Who takes a cab just to go next door?

Oh, right. We'd forgotten. We were talking about the Wicket.

"Are your parents home for this party?" the Wicket said without greeting. "I would so love to see your dear mother again. Perhaps she's inside?"

The Wicket made for the front door.

"No," Annie said, racing to block the front door with her body.

Six of us, all except Petal, raced to Annie's side. There was no way we'd let the Wicket in our house unsupervised. Who knew what she might do?

"The party's out here," Durinda said.

"En*tire*ly out here," Georgia said.

"So if you have to use the bathroom—" Jackie started.

"—we're afraid you'll have to go use your own," Marcia finished.

"You could take a cab there," Rebecca said.

"Would you like us to call one for you now?" Zinnia offered.

Petal would have said something, but she was still busily driving her car. *Beep-beep!*

"Fine," the Wicket said, looking defeated. "I'll stay out here."

She went over to the food table, picked up a blue fork, and began eating her own fruitcake.

"Why don't you start the barbecue, dear?" Mrs. Pete suggested to Pete. "That man who's climbing the walls looks like he might be getting hungry, and that bouncing girl does too."

"Sounds like a plan," Pete said gamely. "What am I barbecuing again?"

"Fish dogs," Mrs. Pete said. "It was Zinnia's idea."

"Ah, right," Pete said, still surprisingly gamely.

He tried to light the grill, but it wouldn't light.

"That's funny," he said. "I'm sure I'm doing it right. The instructions for the matches are right on the bottom. It says clearly 'Close cover and strike match,' and that's what I'm doing here."

"They look like they might be wet," Marcia pointed out.

"That's my fault," Petal said, pulling her car to a stop. "When I saw them on the counter I got scared. Children aren't supposed to play with matches, so I doused them in water. Carl the talking refrigerator helped me; robot Betty too. I hope no one minds too very much. Bye!"

And off Petal went again.

"This *stinks!*" Rebecca said. "Today's supposed to be

a celebration of *me* and now we can't properly barbecue the main course?"

It was then, as Frank Freud climbed the walls and the Wicket ate fruitcake and the McG and the Mr. McG made goo-goo eyes at each other and Mandy bounced and Petal beeped and Will Simms stood there being just-in-general wonderful and the rest of us stood around too, that Rebecca raised both hands in frustration and pointed all ten fingers at the grill.

Fire flew from her fingertips.

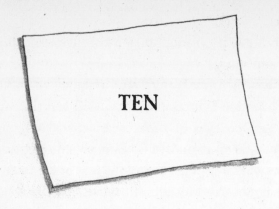

TEN

Fire flew from her fingertips.

You're not imagining things.

Yes, we really did just say that.

And we said it because it's what happened.

The fire that flew from Rebecca's fingers was so powerful that it not only set aflame the previously cold charcoal briquettes but also shot flames toward the sky, like fireworks. When the great fire settled down a bit, we could see that the fish dogs that had been waiting to be cooked had sizzled right down to mere cinders.

Frank Freud, still wearing the wall-walkers, froze against the wall of our house. The Wicket froze with a piece of fruitcake halfway to her mouth. The Mr. McG squeezed the McG's hand tighter. Mandy Stenko stopped bouncing. Will went on being just-in-general wonderful.

"Oh my," Mrs. Pete said.

"Now that's a power," Will said in hushed respect.

"Isn't anyone going to get the fire extinguisher?" Petal said.

Pete put his fingers to his lips and let out a loud whistle, and then he clapped his hands together smartly. We suspected he was trying to get our attention.

"Nothing to see here," he said with forced calm. "Party's over, folks."

"You don't have to tell me twice," Frank Freud said, hurrying down the wall in the wall-walkers.

"Can I borrow your phone to call a cab?" the Wicket asked.

Rebecca turned to the Wicket, outraged. "But you can't call a cab. My party's just getting started!"

Seeing the angry look on Rebecca's face and the way Rebecca was raising her finger to point, the Wicket dropped her fruitcake and began running. "Never mind the cab," the Wicket shouted over her shoulder. "I think I can make it home on my own."

"You'll stay, won't you?" Rebecca said, turning to the McG and the Mr. McG.

"We'd like to," the McG said, and we thought she almost sounded sincere.

"But we just remembered another engagement," the Mr. McG said.

"Plus," the McG added with a glance toward Pete, with whom she'd become somewhat friendly since the time Pete helped us evict Crazy Serena from our lives after Crazy Serena had teachernapped the McG and Eightnapped us, "it looks like you have some family matters to attend to. In private."

And then they were gone too.

"Why did you put an end to my party?" Rebecca said, rounding on Pete in anger, all ten fingers raised.

Pete held a steadying hand out toward her.

"Easy, pet," he said. "I only did it for your own good. There are some things that the fewer outsiders who see it, the better."

"Besides," Durinda said, "the fish dogs have been reduced to cinders, so it's not like we had a main course to serve anyone anyway."

"All we have left are these stupid salads," Georgia said.

"Can we stay?" Will said. "Mandy and me?"

"Is that okay, Mr. Pete?" Jackie asked. "Will and Mandy are mostly insiders, not outsiders."

"Are you sure that's what you want?" Pete asked Will.

"Of course," Will said. "I'd love to see what happens next."

"And how about you, lamb?" Pete asked, turning to Mandy.

Mandy gulped, and we were sure that she was going to ask to call her mother. But then she surprised us.

"I suppose I would like to stay too," she said. "This is kind of fascinating in an I've-never-seen-anything-quite-like-this-before sort of way."

"Is it better than going to Antarctica?" Annie wanted to know.

"Yes," Mandy said, "a bit. So, what happens next?"

"I know this part!" Will said excitedly. "Next we go to the drawing room to read the note about Rebecca getting her power!"

"Well, what are we waiting for?" Mandy said.

Wow, we thought. A minute ago Mandy seemed hesitant to stay, and now she was hurrying us to get on with things.

"That is," Marcia said, for once sounding dark, "if there even is a note this time. The note leaver's been wonky lately."

We ignored her and raced to the drawing room. Even Petal raced. She may have been more petrified of Rebecca than ever, but the notes were always a high point for us.

"Will there be a note or won't there? Will there be a note or won't there?" Marcia kept muttering when we were all standing in front of the loose stone in the drawing room.

"Cut it out," Georgia said. "You sound like you're playing he-loves-me-he-loves-me-not with a daisy. The loose stone is *not* a daisy."

"See if there's a note! See if there's a note!" Zinnia cried with excitement, hands clasped together.

Rebecca slid the loose stone out, and this time, unlike the last time . . .

There was a note back there.

"Read what it says!" Zinnia cried. "Read what it says!"

Rebecca did.

Dear Rebecca,

I always knew you were a fiery girl —
nice work!

"'A fiery girl,'" Rebecca echoed. "I rather like that."

"And I rather like," Marcia said, "that the note leaver is back — yippee!"

Rebecca continued reading.

Thirteen down, three to go.

"But wait," Marcia said. "I think the math is all wrong this time. Rebecca got two powers: superhuman strength and now this fire thing."

"You got superhuman strength too?" Will asked Rebecca, his eyes wide.

"Yes," Rebecca said. "Would you like me to lift something really large for you?"

"I don't think now's the right time for that," Pete said.

"But what can this mean?" Marcia said. "Does the note leaver not realize Rebecca now has two powers? Does the note leaver not know about the superhuman strength?"

"Who cares what the note leaver knows or doesn't know?" Rebecca shrugged.

"I care!" Marcia was outraged.

"So?" Rebecca said. "Maybe it's like I said before. Maybe the superhuman-strength stuff is just me being me and not a power at all."

"Oh no!" Petal cried. "Does this mean that even after July is over, you'll still be Wife-Carrying me?"

We ignored Petal.

"I know one thing it means," Zinnia said.

Now this was shocking: Zinnia saying she knew what something meant without first claiming that one of the cats told her in one of her imaginary Zinnia-to-kitty conversations.

"It means," Zinnia said, "that Rebecca has managed to hog two powers instead of the usual one." Zinnia crossed her arms, and her lower lip came out. "I suppose when my month finally arrives there won't even be one single power left for me, not even a measly one."

"Oh, I'm sure that won't be the case," Durinda said, placing an arm around Zinnia's shoulders.

"Of course not," Jackie said, placing an arm around Zinnia's shoulders from the other side. "I'm sure you'll get a fine power and probably the best present anyone's had yet."

Zinnia was slightly mollified by all the hugging, but not much. "We'll see about that," she said glumly.

"Does anyone else see there's a P.S. at the bottom of Rebecca's letter?" Mandy asked.

"A P.S.?" Zinnia zoomed straight from glum to excited again. "I don't know if we've ever had one of those before. Have we?"

"That's funny," Annie said, rubbing her chin as though she expected to find a fake beard there even though she'd only ever worn a fake mustache. "Right now I can't remember if we have or not."

"I hope it's not bad news," Petal said.

"Read it! Read it!" Zinnia shouted at Rebecca.

"Perhaps if you'd stop shouting," Rebecca said. "Oh, fine."

P.S. Remember, Rebecca: Always use your power for good, not evil.

"*Ha!*" Rebecca said, crumpling up the note. "What

a silly note leaver. Of course I'm going to use my power for evil. Why, this is just the beginning of my world domination. I think when I'm done, I'll rename whatever country we live in Rebeccaland. Or maybe I'll rename the whole planet that. The universe even!"

"Well, you'd better hurry up and dominate then," Georgia said. "July's over in seventeen days, and with it goes your power."

"You're right," Rebecca said, a dark gleam entering her eye. It was the darkest gleam we'd ever seen there. It scared us all, even Annie. "I'll need to begin right away. Now, what should I set on fire first so I can dominate it . . ."

Rebecca left the room then, her ten fingers outstretched menacingly; we could only imagine that she was looking for something to burn and that wherever her cat, Rambunctious, was, the cat had probably set something on fire too. We hoped the cats had their own fire extinguisher. We were certainly going to need ours.

"Did anyone else notice that the note wasn't signed?" Mandy asked.

"They never are," Will informed her.

"How rude!" Mandy said.

We ignored Mandy.

"What does this mean?" Petal asked fearfully.

"Which part?" Annie asked.

"All Rebecca's talk about using her power to do that dominate thing she mentioned," Petal said. "What does it all mean?"

"Power corrupts," Pete said, "and absolute power corrupts absolutely."

"That's not helpful," Petal cried. "Because I don't know what *that* means either!"

We weren't sure we understood it completely, but we had the feeling that whatever happened next, it was going to be worse, much worse than Rebecca carrying Petal around the front yard.

"I think what Mr. Pete is trying to say," Jackie said, "is that Rebecca has become absolutely corrupted."

Oh dear. That couldn't be good.

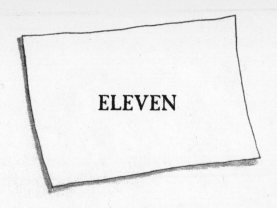

ELEVEN

"Perhaps it won't be that bad," we said to ourselves as we stood in the drawing room wondering what Rebecca was up to.

"Perhaps it won't be that bad," we said to ourselves as we went to sleep that night, Mandy and Will long gone.

At least we didn't smell anything burning.

But the next morning, not long after we arose, it began to dawn on us that, yes, it really was going to be that bad.

"What do you mean," Rebecca demanded of Durinda, "you've made chocolate chip pancakes for breakfast? Didn't you get the memo I left you last night saying I wanted pink frosting for breakfast from now on?"

"What memo?" Durinda asked.

"Okay," Rebecca said. "Perhaps I forgot to leave one because I was too busy making a list of the things I need to burn down in order to take over the world. Still . . ."

And Rebecca raised her ten fingers, pointed them at the dining-room table, on which lay ten servings of chocolate chip pancakes, and let fly with her power.

A moment later, the table was engulfed in flames.

"See?" Petal said. "I told you children shouldn't be allowed to play with fire, but does anyone ever listen to me? Oh, no. All you people ever say is 'Poor Petal, what a crazy girl with all her silly little worries that never amount to anything.' Well?"

That was odd. It almost sounded as though Petal were angry and standing up for herself.

"I was hungry," Annie said.

"Couldn't you have waited," Georgia complained, "until after we'd eaten to set fire to the dining-room table?"

"Those flames are shooting rather high," Marcia observed.

"I'll go get the fire extinguisher," Zinnia offered.

"Well, I'm hungry too," Rebecca said angrily, raising her fingers again.

"Wait right here," Jackie said before Rebecca could do anything with those ten fingers. "I'll go get you a can of pink frosting."

In what seemed like a second, certainly much faster than it would have taken any of us, Jackie was back with the can.

"Here you go," she offered, extending the can to Rebecca along with a spoon.

"Why don't you watch some TV?" Durinda suggested soothingly to Rebecca as Zinnia sprayed the fire extinguisher at the table, replacing flame with foam.

We wondered about Durinda using that soothing voice. Yes, Durinda was soothing by nature, just as Georgia was anti-soothing. But it seemed to us that for most of July, she'd been annoyed with Rebecca. Then it hit us. Rebecca was carrying ten lethal weapons now, and Durinda was wisely choosing not to rock the boat.

"That's not a bad idea," Rebecca said. "Maybe if I watch TV I'll get some more world-taking-over ideas."

"So what shall we have for breakfast instead?" Annie asked once Rebecca was gone.

"I don't feel like cooking pancakes a second time," Durinda said.

"Besides," Marcia said observantly, "we no longer have a dining-room table to eat them on."

"How about Razzle Crunchies?" Jackie suggested. "That's always easy."

"I like Razzle Crunchies," Zinnia said, having finished with extinguishing the table. "They razzle. And they crunch."

"We don't even need a table to eat them at," Georgia said. "We can just put them in bowls and go eat them in the TV room, like uncivilized people."

"Razzle Crunchies it is," Durinda said.

Soon we were all gathered in the TV room, even the Petes, eating Razzle Crunchies and watching Rebecca change the channels with the remote.

"Blast!" Rebecca cried at the TV. "There's nothing helpful on!"

What Rebecca did then was worse than what robot Betty had done, grinding Razzle Crunchies into the carpet when she didn't like what was going on in that late-night movie.

"So much for having a TV in the house," Annie said as we watched flames shoot back at us from the middle of what was once our television set.

"Well," Pete said with surprising calm, "it's probably for the best. They say that TV rots the brain."

"Who is *they*?" Georgia said.

"I suppose we'll never know about the brain-rotting thing," Marcia said, "now that we no longer have a TV."

Georgia sighed. "I would have liked to know what it's like to have a rotting brain."

"Do you people *see* what I mean?" Petal said.

"I'll go get the fire extinguisher," Zinnia said.

As Zinnia exited the room, we saw Zither hurry by the open doorway with a tiny fire extinguisher on her back. We wondered where she was going. Perhaps Zinnia would ask her.

That almost made us laugh. The idea of Zinnia thinking she could communicate with the cats — that got us every time. *As if.*

Still, we hoped her imaginary conversation with her

cat didn't take too long. The whole room could catch fire in the meantime.

"Rebecca," Jackie suggested, "while we, er, clean up in here, why don't you go into one of the seasonal rooms and play for a bit?"

Playing for a bit in one of the seasonal rooms—that sounded like a good idea. Playing for a bit could calm any person down, even Rebecca. Jackie was always coming up with good ideas.

And this would have been a good idea if Rebecca had chosen to go to Winter or Summer or Spring. It would have been a good idea if Jackie had thought sooner than she did to shout after Rebecca, "Just don't go in Fall!"

As it was, Jackie's shout came too late.

Fall was always so dry, being Fall of course, with all the things that went with Fall. Fall was the driest room in the house. Really, Fall was just one big conflagration waiting to happen.

We arrived at the doorway of Fall to see the entire room ablaze.

"Oh dear," Rebecca said, at last looking awed at her own power.

"Oh, this is very bad," Petal said. "Rebecca chose me to show off her strength. What if she chooses me for this too?"

"It'll be like the Salem witch trials," Annie said.

"But without a real witch," Georgia added.

"I'll go get the fire extinguisher," Zinnia offered, sounding as though she might be growing weary of it all.

"Psst," Pete whispered to us as Rebecca went on staring at what she'd done. "I think we need to have a family conference."

"Without Rebecca," Mrs. Pete added.

Pete had used the term *family conference*. We were inclined to feel moved by this, the idea that even though we weren't related to them by blood, the Petes thought of us as family. But we had no time to be sentimental.

"You're right," Annie said. "Things simply can't go on like this."

* * * * * * * *

We held our family conference standing around the charred remains of our dining-room table. We would have sat, but the chairs had been destroyed too. So stand we did around the smoldering mess.

Rebecca was upstairs lying down for a bit, having been instructed by Annie to do so.

"That's a good idea," Rebecca had said when Annie suggested it. "I think better when I'm horizontal, so I'll be able to come up with more world-taking-over ideas."

"Things simply can't go on like this," Annie said again now.

We saw that Annie was right.

We'd suffered threats from outside before, many times: the Wicket, Crazy Serena, Frank Freud, Crazy Serena again. But this time the threat was coming from within. Would Rebecca destroy our house and us in it?

She might not mean to, but she was certainly capable of it.

"We need to find a way to contain Rebecca's power until August hits," Pete said.

"But how?" Mrs. Pete said.

"Perhaps we could tie Rebecca's hands behind her back," Petal suggested.

We suspected that Petal had been wanting to do this to Rebecca for a very long time.

"She'd only shoot fire backwards," Marcia said.

"And then where would we be?" Georgia said. "With Rebecca unable to see what she was shooting fire at, who knows what she might set on fire by mistake?"

"I wish a carrier pigeon would come to visit," Durinda said with a sigh. "Especially if the carrier pigeon came bearing a note with helpful advice."

That seemed like a too-magical thing to wish for, that a carrier pigeon would just appear with useful information at exactly the right moment. Still, we couldn't blame Durinda as we gazed at the windows hopefully and then wistfully. It would have been nice.

"We could wrap Rebecca's hands in great big mitts so that her fingers were covered," Petal suggested.

"I don't think that would work either," Annie said. "Unless the mitts were made of steel, Rebecca could shoot fire right through them."

"You're right," Pete said. "What we need is something that will remove Rebecca completely from the house."

"You mean like send her to jail?" Petal suggested.

We all ignored Petal, except for Pete.

"Unless the jail's made entirely of steel," he said, "that wouldn't work either."

"Steel . . . steel . . . steel . . ." Marcia mused. "People keep mentioning steel. I'm guessing there might be something in that."

"We need something completely made out of steel," Annie said excitedly.

"And then we need to put something into the thing made out of steel so that Rebecca will enter it," Jackie said.

"Whatever this is we're thinking of," Zinnia said, "it sounds like it might be a mean trick to play on a person." Then Zinnia sighed. "But I am getting tired of hauling that fire extinguisher around. My back is killing me. Zither says hers is too."

"Do you think you could build something like that,

Mr. Pete?" Annie asked. "Like what we're describing?"

"Yes, I think I can," Pete said. "And as hard as it might be, the idea of sequestering one of you lot, it has to be done."

"What does *sequestering* mean?" Petal asked.

"It means to keep someone apart from other people," Jackie said.

Okay, we'd known about Jackie, but who knew Pete had such a vast vocabulary?

"It's not just for our own good and the good of society," Pete went on. "It's for Rebecca's good as well. Why, if we just let her go on like this, she might eventually go up in self-immolation."

Six of us weren't completely sure what that meant but we were fairly certain Pete meant that Rebecca might set herself on fire.

Conflagration. Immolation.

One good thing that was coming out of all this: we were expanding our knowledge of synonyms for the word *fire*.

At least there was that.

* * * * * * * *

"What are you doing, Mr. Pete?" Rebecca asked.

Rebecca had apparently grown tired of being horizontal and was now back to being vertical. She'd found us in the backyard, gathered around Pete as he worked.

Pete grabbed a six-inch-thick sheet of reinforced steel and placed it next to another. Without being asked, Petal handed him a steel nail.

"Oh, what a shame," Pete said. "You've spoiled the surprise. Why, I'm building something for you, Rebecca."

"For me?" Rebecca said. "But why? And what is it?"

"I'm doing it because you saved my life," Pete said. "As for what it is, just watch and see."

So we all watched, most of us knowing what Pete was building, one of us not.

At last, Pete was done with the small structure; it looked kind of like Daddy's toolshed, only made out of steel.

"I still don't understand what it is or what it's for," Rebecca said. "I don't know why there's a little rectangular slot in the door, as if someone wanted to make sure there was proper ventilation, or what the fluffy pillow is doing in there, or why there's a sink with a water glass and toothbrush in it, or why you installed a toilet in the corner. And what's that miniature version of it doing off to one side and why does it have a water dish and a soft cushion and a catnip toy and a litter box inside of it?"

"Why," Pete said, "that's for Rambunctious. Rambunctious deserves a prize too."

According to prior arrangement, Durinda, Georgia, Jackie, Marcia, Petal, and Zinnia disappeared then, soon reappearing with wheelbarrows piled high with cans of pink frosting and kibble.

Immediately we began stocking the shelves inside the two steel structures.

"What—" Rebecca started to say, but Pete cut her off.

"It's your prize," Pete said. "I know how much you like pink frosting so I wanted to put a whole bunch of it separate from the house so you'd never have to share again with anyone else, never run out. And of course Rambunctious has her own personal supply of kibble now too."

Rambunctious tiptoed on cat feet into the smaller of the two steel things Pete had created.

"This is magnificent!" Rebecca said, entering the larger structure. "This is—"

That's when we slammed both doors shut.

And bolted them.

* * * * * * * *

"Let me out of here!" Rebecca shouted.

Sounds of a cat wailing came from the smaller structure.

"Zither says Rambunctious would like to be let out too," Zinnia informed us.

We ignored Zinnia. A person didn't have to pretend to have the ability to communicate with cats to understand Rebecca's cat's sentiments at the moment.

"We will," Durinda shouted back to Rebecca.

"On August first," Jackie added.

"When it's safe to be around you again," Petal said. Then she paused, finally adding, "Or saf*er*."

"It's for your own good," Pete said.

Fire flew out the rectangular slots on the doors of both structures, but we ignored the flames, and the continued shouting too.

"Shall we go inside where it's quieter?" Annie said.

"I'll make us a snack," Durinda said.

"Oh, good," Zinnia said. "After all this, I've really built up an appetite."

"I think I'll stay out here," Georgia said, "maybe lounge in the hammock."

"Won't all the shouting bother you?" Marcia asked.

"Nah," Georgia said. "I find racket to be rather peaceful."

"Just stay out of the way of the flames," Jackie advised.

"Is everyone else ready for that snack now?" Mrs. Pete said.

So that's what we did.

We went and had a snack, feeling as though life had returned to some semblance of normal.

And for the next seven days, we continued to do normal things. We cleaned out the worst of the damage to Fall. We got the long picnic table we'd used at the Bastille Day party and put it in the dining room, so we had something to stand around when we ate our meals. We even went out and purchased a new TV.

We weren't worried so much about our brains rotting. We always seemed to have bigger things to worry about.

It was a peaceful week filled with us taking turns lying in the hammock, drinking lemonade and lying on our backs staring up at the puffy clouds to see animal shapes in them, all of which the Mr. McG had once advised us to do over the summer.

We didn't even mind, while we were relaxing outdoors, hearing the sounds of Rebecca shouting and Rambunctious doing the kitty equivalent of shouting and seeing flames flying through those rectangular slots. It'd been our experience in life that people could get used to almost anything.

Or at least we could.

* * * * * * * *

On the seventh day of Rebecca's sequestration, a strange thing happened.

Rebecca stopped shouting.

Could Rebecca have finally run out of anger? That hardly seemed possible. Whatever the case, Rebecca had stopped shouting and instead was speaking—dare we say it?—calmly.

How eerie.

"If I tell you what I've figured out," Rebecca said quietly through the slot to us when we went out to say good morning to her, as we did every morning, "and I further promise not to use my power again unless necessary, will you let me out of here?"

"It's a trick!" Petal cried.

"No, it's not," Rebecca said, still eerily calm.

"What do you mean, what you've 'figured out'?" Annie said.

"About Queen and the Ochos," Rebecca said. "Also about the Wicket and Frank Freud and Crazy Serena. You know, stuff like that." Rebecca paused. "It's amazing what a person can figure out in her own head if she's given time and space to think about things."

This was a revelation. We'd had good evidence that the only things filling Rebecca's mind were spider webs and cans of pink frosting. We never would have guessed there were actual ideas up there.

But wait a second. Hang on.

Rebecca now *knew* things?

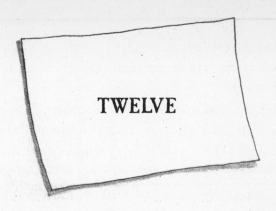

TWELVE

"I don't hear any of you talking," Rebecca said after a long moment of silence. "Fine," she said when we still didn't say anything. "I'll tell you what I know and then you decide if it was worth enough to trust me and let me out of here."

A moment passed.

"You do have our attention now," Annie said to the slot. "Please talk."

"It's like this," Rebecca began. "We've already figured out that Queen is Mommy's identical twin sister, a sister we never knew about for some reason, just like we never knew about Crazy Serena. And we figured out that the Ochos are Queen's children because her last name is Ocho and we know there are children involved. But what we haven't figured out, at least not before today, is how many children there are."

"And you've managed to figure this out?" Georgia said with sneering skepticism.

"Yes," Rebecca said, and there was that calm again, serenity even. "There are eight Ochos, just like there are eight Huits."

"Eight?" Petal cried in fear. "So many?"

"Yes," Rebecca said. "It stands to reason, doesn't it?" She paused. "The Eights? That's what we're called. The Other Eights? That's what they were called in all those notes the carrier pigeons brought us. Eight isn't just our last name, and it can't be just their last name. Eight is how many of us there are. Eight must be how many of them there are too."

Wow. The idea of there being eight Ochos, just like we were eight Huits. Eight Ochos who were . . . our cousins!

"I can't believe I'm saying this," Annie said, "but I think Rebecca's right."

"I'm sure she's right," Marcia said. "It's simple mathematical math sense."

"Have you figured out anything else about the Ochos?" Jackie asked Rebecca.

"Not for certain," Rebecca said. "But I see no reason why they can't be octuplets too."

What a horrifying thought! We'd always thought we were so original!

"They could be octuplet girls, for all we know," Rebecca said, "just like us. Or maybe they're even boys—

our male counterparts. But whatever they are, I'm certain there are eight of them."

This was so much to think about.

"But wait a second," Annie said. "You also said you'd figured out something about the Wicket, Frank Freud, and Crazy Serena."

"Oh, that," Rebecca said, as though it were nothing.

"Yes, that," Georgia prompted.

"I simply figured out," Rebecca said, "that we need to stop worrying about them like we always do. None of them knows anything. If they did, it would be obvious. All they want is the secret of eternal life. We should forget about them and refocus our energies on discovering where Mommy and Daddy disappeared to."

"Don't you mean to add 'or how they died'?" Georgia said.

"No, I don't," Rebecca said. "I'm sure they're still alive. I feel it."

This was a new Rebecca.

"Can I come out now?" Rebecca said. "I promise not to burn things unless you specifically ask me to."

What else could we do? We let her out. Rambunctious too. We weren't sure they'd behave, but Rebecca had promised, and Zinnia informed us that Rambunctious had promised too. Letting them out after their promises — it was a chance we'd have to take.

* * * * * * * *

"Well, what do you know?" Rebecca said calmly as she reached for the knob on the front door. "It looks like my gift has arrived."

Rebecca was right once more, we realized as we saw the heart-shaped locket dangling from the doorknob.

"What are you going to put inside it?" Zinnia asked when Rebecca opened it and we saw there was nothing inside except two empty spaces for pictures.

"I'm not sure yet," Rebecca said, slipping it over her head. "I'll have to give it some thought."

Rebecca giving something some thought? This was such a new Rebecca, we didn't know what to do with her!

"I think I'll go check and see if my note's here," Rebecca said, heading off to the drawing room.

We followed her.

Sure enough, Rebecca was right . . . again!

Dear Rebecca,

Fourteen down, two to go. I must say, with
you involved, it was touch-and-go if this
day would ever arrive. Good show.

"Aren't you going to get mad at the note?" Georgia
said. "It sounds to me like the note was insulting you,
with all that stuff about 'with you involved.'"

"I'm not bothered by it," Rebecca said. "The note
seems to know me pretty well."

This Rebecca was so new and so confusing to poor
Petal that of course Petal fainted.

* * * * * * * *

The rest of the month passed with the household oddly
serene; Rebecca kept her word and did not set anything
else on fire.

On the last day, which was a Thursday, Pete offered
to take us all out to dinner as a treat.

"Are you sure?" Annie asked. "That could get ex-
pensive."

"Mostly," Georgia said, "when restaurants see us coming, restaurants run the other way."

"I could use a night off from the kitchen," Durinda said.

"I'm sure," Pete said.

"Don't you ever work anymore?" Marcia asked Pete. "I'm not complaining, but I have noticed that you do seem to be around all the time since you moved in."

"I just think that maybe you need me a bit more than you used to," Pete said.

"You need us more," Mrs. Pete added, "which is why we've stayed on."

"Shall we go?" Pete said.

* * * * * * * *

We arrived at the restaurant and told the person there that we needed a table for ten, and eventually we settled into our seats.

"This is such a treat!" Zinnia said, giddy.

We ignored her.

"I decided what to put in my locket," Rebecca said.

"What?" Jackie asked.

"Pictures of Mommy and Daddy," Rebecca said, opening the locket to show us. "It's to remind myself not to worry so much about the little stuff and to keep my mind focused on what's really important."

We all got tears in our eyes at that, even Pete.

"I've been thinking," Marcia said when we'd all recovered, "and what I've been thinking is that this month has been the oddest month yet."

"You mean because of Rebecca basically getting two powers?" Jackie asked.

"Marcia, are you still obsessing about the note leaver?" Georgia said.

"Those things too," Marcia said, "but that's not what I meant."

"Then what did you mean?" Annie asked.

"It's just that when others of us have gotten our powers, we've somehow used our powers to help save the day," Marcia said. "But unless I missed something, Rebecca only ever used her power of fire to destroy things."

"I don't know if it's so strange." Rebecca shrugged. "That week I spent in the steel structure, all that time I had to think and to gain knowledge about stuff..." Rebecca shrugged again. "Sure, power is power. But knowledge is an even greater power."

That sounded so ... wise.

This Rebecca was so new, our heads were spinning!

At last, the waitress arrived to take our drinks order.

"Mango juice for all the others, please," Rebecca ordered before anyone else had the chance to.

"And for you?" the waitress asked.

"A giant glass of pulp, please," Rebecca said, her grin splitting across her face. "The biggest glass of pulp you've got."

Then, for good measure, Rebecca rose from her seat, threw her napkin on the table, and shouted at Petal, "I'm going to Wife-Carry you!"

As Rebecca chased Petal through the restaurant and Petal shrieked in what could have been panic or could have been glee, Zinnia rose from her seat. And then Zinnia began spinning happily where she stood, joyfully crying out, "Yay! Tomorrow's August first. *Finally.* Me next!"

It was a good night.